I0773160

NO ROGUE LIKE YOU

ROGUES OF REDEMPTION, BOOK 3

BY

BRENNA ASH

© Copyright 2024 by Brenna Ash
Text by Brenna Ash
Cover by Dar Albert

Dragonblade Publishing, Inc. is an imprint of Kathryn Le Veque Novels, Inc.
P.O. Box 23
Moreno Valley, CA 92556
ceo@dragonbladepublishing.com

Produced in the United States of America

First Edition September 2024
Trade Paperback Edition

Reproduction of any kind except where it pertains to short quotes in relation to advertising or promotion is strictly prohibited.

All Rights Reserved.

The characters and events portrayed in this book are fictitious. Any similarity to real persons, living or dead, is purely coincidental and not intended by the author.

ARE YOU SIGNED UP FOR DRAGONBLADE'S BLOG?

You'll get the latest news and information on exclusive giveaways, exclusive excerpts, coming releases, sales, free books, cover reveals and more.

Check out our complete list of authors, too!

No spam, no junk. That's a promise!

Sign Up Here

www.dragonbladepublishing.com

Dearest Reader;

Thank you for your support of a small press. At Dragonblade Publishing, we strive to bring you the highest quality Historical Romance from some of the best authors in the business. Without your support, there is no 'us', so we sincerely hope you adore these stories and find some new favorite authors along the way.

Happy Reading!

CEO, Dragonblade Publishing

Additional Dragonblade Books by Author Brenna Ash

Rogues of Redemption Series
Sweet Rogue O' Mine (Book 1)
Rogue You Like a Hurricane (Book 2)
No Rogue Like You (Book 3)

CHAPTER ONE

Edinburgh, 1816

FINLAY PRIMROSE WAS never one for garden parties, or any party really. But yet, such a gathering is where the Earl of Rosebery currently found himself. Duty mandated his attendance, not want.

He surveyed the well-manicured grounds as he sipped the champagne he had snatched from one of the trays being carried by the staff of the Duke of Forthington. An old acquaintance whose wife had insisted on this party to celebrate the recent birth of their son.

He masked a grimace as the liquid bubbled down his throat. There was a time when he enjoyed the effervescence of champagne, but he much preferred whisky now. Though neither did anything to cool him from the heat of the sun. Why did they always insist on having these parties at the peak of day?

Fingal, Finlay's twin brother, and his wife, Yvette, were nowhere in sight and Finlay breathed a sigh of relief. After all, his ne'er-do-well brother was one of the reasons Finlay was even here. Their late father was the other, with his ridiculous demand that Finlay wed before his next birthday—or lose the title to his younger brother. It would be a devastating turn of events for such a thing to come to fruition. Especially with how irresponsible his brother was.

He would not allow such a travesty to happen. Once again, for the umpteenth time, he found himself cursing his father and his damned will. What kind of person included such a clause? A person who still wanted to rule his sons' lives even from the grave, that's what kind.

"My lord," Lady Ruddiman interrupted his thoughts.

He rolled his lips inward to stop a biting remark to tell her that he had no interest in what she was about to offer. Which was most likely the lass dragging her feet behind her mother who, as if on a mission, trudged toward him. This very scenario was why he usually avoided these types of gatherings. Instead, he bowed politely and gave the woman a half-hearted smile that he didn't feel.

Taking no notice of his disinterest, the buxom woman curtsied in return, her hair piled so haphazardly high on her head, he feared it might topple over. Blonde ringlets fell in front of each ear. Emeralds encased in gold dangled and swayed back and forth from her earlobes with each step she took.

"May I introduce ye to my daughter?" She tugged on the gloved hand of the lass cowering behind her. The lass stumbled forward, her cheeks pink with embarrassment as she caught her footing. "Miss Cordelia Ruddiman," Lady Ruddiman said proudly, a huge smile plastered on her overly powdered face, made more prominent by the harsh red rouge she had rubbed onto her cheeks.

To her credit, the lass acted through the steps that she had no doubt been taught for years now, preparing her for her introduction into society. She dipped into a curtsy and looked up at him through lowered lashes.

The lass was pleasant enough. Unlike her mother, her blonde hair was perfectly coiffed. Her cheeks perfectly rouged. Lips perfectly tinted. She could be what he was looking for in a wife.

But her smile did not reach her eyes. Her persona far too meek. It was as if she wanted to be anywhere but where they were. Which he could appreciate. That was more than likely the one and only sentiment they shared.

He cleared his throat and bowed his acknowledgement. "'Tis

lovely to meet ye, Miss Ruddiman. I do hope ye are enjoying your afternoon."

"Aye, my lord. Verra much so."

As she spoke, Finlay noted the waver in her voice. The falter in her smile as she looked up at him. Aye, her attendance was most definitely not her idea. Unfortunately for her, it seemed marrying off her daughter was what was most important to Lady Ruddiman. Her daughter's unwillingness to be committed to a man mattered naught.

Finlay felt bad for the poor lass. He had seen enough young women enter into society and he kenned it was not easy. Some lasses handled it better than others. But being forced into it before one was ready struck him as unwarranted and a bit cruel.

Miss Ruddiman appeared young in both mind and age. The lass could not be more than ten and seven. Which was much too young for him and far from what he was looking for. He wanted a wife that had some spark to her. A wife that would challenge him. Not one that would just bend and break to whatever he said. Which was what Miss Ruddiman would surely do.

Though he had no interest in Miss Ruddiman, he was sure she would find a match this season—just not with him.

Not wanting to engage in more conversation or open the door for future enquiries, he excused himself and walked to the outer perimeter of the garden, staying away from the crowd, deftly avoiding meeting the eyes of the den of lionesses trying to marry off their daughters to him or one of the other eligible bachelors in attendance. He tugged on his cravat, tilting his head to the side and took a deep breath. He was beginning to feel like an animal in a cage. He longed for the solace of his study. But hiding away at his estate would not get him what he needed.

Two months. That was when he turned twenty-eight. By that time, he needed to be married. If not, Fingal became earl and Finlay refused to let that happen. His twin had never shown any interest in the Primrose family affairs, whether it be their holdings or their finances. Instead he focused all his interest in whoring his way through the city—until he had found his wife and even still he wouldn't be surprised if Fingal still had dalliances while continuing to burn his way through the family fortune. His brother had nearly failed out of Eton, for God's sake. He would have if their father had not stepped in with a sizeable donation to the school. How that in itself didn't stop their father from putting his ridiculous plan forward, he would never understand.

Money was not an issue for the Primroses. But that did not mean that Fingal would not set them on a path of destruction. Even the greatest houses could fall under the right circumstances.

Fingal Primrose and his new wife were the last people that Rosewood Manor needed. Yvette was a nice enough lass, but had no sense when it came to financial affairs. They hadn't been married long and Finlay wasn't entirely convinced that she wasn't only after the Rosebery fortune. She spent money as if it came from unlimited resources. So much so, that Finlay had had to put a limit to their monthly allowance. Something that his brother hated him for.

Their father be damned. He surely must have been daft when he came up with this hare-brained idea. That was the only conclusion Finlay could come to. Their father had to ken that turning the title and all of its holdings over to Fingal and Yvette would be the downfall of them all.

Nay. He would not allow it to happen. He refused to. If finding a wife was what Finlay needed to do to satisfy their father's last wishes, then find a wife he would. Doing so would also lessen Fingal's claim to the title. His brother thought that since he was married, he was better suited to be earl.

How hard could finding a wife be? Lasses had never been an issue for him. He'd lost himself in the warm body of many a lass over the years. This really shouldn't be any different.

He glanced over his shoulder at the pool of mothers and daughters in search of titled and fitting husbands and he shook his head.

It should be an easy endeavor—there were plenty of available lasses at this party alone—if he cared naught for the type of woman he would be bonded to. But he unfortunately, did. If he was going to be forced to marry, he wanted to have some interest in the lass. Turning the corner he sought the solace of the maze where he knew benches were set that he could sit upon and gather his head for a moment. Jumping into this pit of venomous snakes was going to take a lot of patience. A trait that Finlay was severely lacking these days, the looming deadline hanging over his head a large contributing factor to his disquietude.

He hurried his pace to ensure no one would see his retreat. It reminded him of dashing through enemy lines as he sought safety on the other side. If he recalled correctly, the maze was just on the other side of the brick wall. He rounded the corner and oomph.

A warm, soft body collided into his with a small cry.

Throwing out his arms to steady the lass, his breath caught in his throat as eyes the color of midnight locked with his.

LADY WILLAMINA WATSON had not heard the man approach on the other side of the wall and was only made aware of his presence when her face was pressed against a massive, hard chest, attached to strong arms that had reached out to steady her.

Ice-blue eyes clashed with hers, his blond brows furrowed with concern.

"Sir, my apologies." She stepped back, out of reach of the warm hands that had gripped her arms, causing a frisson of excitement to set her skin afire.

"Are ye hurt?" His deep voice sent shivers rippling up and down her spine.

"Nay. I fear my mind was preoccupied instead of paying attention to where I was walking."

A fierce look blanketed his handsome face as he tilted his

head to look behind her. "Is something amiss?"

Shaking her head, she tried to maneuver around the man, but he stepped in her path, stopping her escape.

"Are ye alone?"

A simple question, but yet not really.

She was, in fact, alone. In more ways than one. Was he asking out of interest? Or did he have sinister thoughts in mind? She doubted the latter. Not with the reaction he had when he thought she might be in danger.

His actions were gallant. Especially since they were strangers.

She was a horrible liar. Every time she attempted a deception her cheeks would flush, giving her away, so she spoke the truth. Soon enough it would become obvious that no one accompanied her anyway.

Straightening her shoulders, she jutted her chin out, trying to show a strong countenance, like she always attended parties on her own. She supposed that was true now that she no longer had a husband, though her cousin did drag her to this particular event. "I am. I was just returning to the party."

He looked over his shoulder.

And she was aware that on this side of the wall, no one could see them.

When his gaze returned to her, she was once again taken aback at how handsome the man was. Blond hair, cut to the latest style, swept back off his forehead. A jawline so precise it looked as if it were cut from the strongest steel. But his eyes were what captured her attention. The palest of blue framed by long light brown lashes. Dare she say he was one of the most fetching men she had ever seen?

Aye, she dared.

"Ye shouldna be out here alone," he stated, his voice low.

Tilting her head to the side, she addressed him. "It doesna appear that I am alone any longer does it, Lord..." she let the sentence go unfinished. She had not the faintest idea of who this man was.

Awareness dawned on his face. "'Twould seem 'tis my turn to apologize as it appears I have forgotten my manners. Lord Primrose. Finlay Primrose." He bent at the waist and gave her a sweeping bow before straightening. "'Tis a pleasure to make your acquaintance…"

As Willamina had done previously, Lord Primrose let the sentence hang in the air as he waited for an answer.

"Willamina Watson." She dipped into a curtsy.

"A lovely name for a lovely lass."

Her cheeks heated. Was he flirting with her? She did not ken. It was a practice completely foreign to her. "Thank ye, my lord."

His gaze remained transfixed on her, not in a leering way. She had had her fair share of those looks since the death of her husband and she found those most unwanted. Those stares made her very uncomfortable. Lord Primrose's stare was the opposite of leering. Was it curiosity? Interest?

Wanting, mayhap?

The longer Lord Primrose looked at her with heat in his gaze, the warmer her skin felt and the more active the flutter of butterflies in her stomach. Or was she imagining it because her body had never experienced such flights of fancy? A reaction she had never had for her late husband. Never once in three short months of a one-sided marriage to her husband had she felt such a strong stirring of excitement that the stranger standing before her had elicited.

An arranged marriage that at first she had wanted no part of. But she had tried her best to be a good and loyal wife. Even though it felt as if she were always fighting against the current of the vicious waves of the ocean. Like she would be swept out to sea if she stopped trying.

However, Gerard had no interest in their marriage or her in general, which he had made obvious by the constant string of women he had brazenly paraded through the halls of their home. 'Twas humiliating. And while her late husband had his many faults, he did not deserve to die at such a young age.

Even with his mistreatment of her and his lack of reciprocation of feelings of adoration, she did love him. And as she went through her time of mourning, her feelings didn't change. She missed him. It mattered naught that he would not react the same had the situation been reversed and it be she that had perished.

Lord Primrose cleared his throat, drawing her attention from the past and back to him. "Are ye certain ye are well, Miss Watson?" He asked, concern darkening his eyes ever so slightly. "Ye look a wee pale."

Willamina found herself taken aback by his intuitiveness, amazed that he could read her so well after just making her acquaintance. She nodded, unable to speak.

"I do no' believe anyone has seen us. I shall remain here for a time while ye rejoin the other guests so as no' to raise any suspicion. I dinna want to cause ye any scandal by being seen alone with me."

She bit back a chuckle at his insinuation.

He cocked his head to the side, a blond brow raised in question.

Where she was from, scandal was her middle name.

CHAPTER TWO

As Willamina hurried from the maze, several times she had to stop herself from looking back to see if Lord Primrose was watching her rejoin the party. Truth be told, she would much rather spend the evening with him than making the rounds with people she did not know.

Her cousin, Gil, had insisted she attend and try to integrate herself into Edinburgh society. She only listened to him because he currently controlled her assets now that she was a widow. Immediately after Gerard died, her father had taken over whatever holdings and coffers Gerard had owned. That arrangement worked well, and her father had afforded her the freedom to live alone, but since the untimely death of both her mother and father, her fate now rested in the hands of her cousin.

Unfortunately, Gil was not of the same inclination to let her do as she pleased. Instead of allowing her to remain at home in Inverness, he demanded she move to his estate in Edinburgh.

She curtsied at a man that bowed in her direction and lifted a glass of champagne from an offered tray.

Of course, that was not her only reason for leaving Inverness. Her name was quite popular there in the gossip sheets and scandal seemed to follow her after Gerard's death.

Surveying the crowd scattered across the vast manicured lawn, she wondered if any of the women would be interested in attending a seance? She would have to convince Gil to host one first though.

Unlikely, considering that was why she found herself in her current predicament. Back in Inverness, she had hosted multiple seances. She found them fascinating. Mediums that proclaimed they could talk to loved ones that have passed caught her interest.

Hosting them had become a joy and she had had many women enjoy her parties and the psychics she hired to entertain them. And that they did. She was happy to play a part in connecting them to their lost loved ones. To see the medium passing on messages, stating that those who had passed were at peace, and not to miss them, they would meet once again.

It was all so enthralling, even if they could never connect her with her own lost loved ones. She supposed that meant they had moved on and were too happy in their afterlives to take time to communicate with the living. In the end, that was all she wished for them.

Willamina continued through the crowd, sipping her champagne, trying to mask her grimace. The bubbly drink was too dry for her taste. She much preferred sweeter wines, but she would drink it, nonetheless.

The women in Inverness were grateful to her for bringing such information to them—until they were not.

She supposed she only had herself to blame. Wanting to bring in someone different, she thought it would add some more excitement to the seance. She should have known better. All it did was ruin her reputation and cause her friends to shun her.

How was she to know the woman was a scam artist? In all of the gatherings she had hosted before that one, and of all the mediums she had hired, none of them were fake. But her last party?

It proved to be a disaster.

Clearly, when the woman stated she was psychic and could see things from beyond the grave, it was malarkey. Knocking on Willamina's door, wearing a ghastly bright orange gown. Well, not really a gown. More like a covering. It was huge and billowy, with gold threads sewn into it in swirling spirals. Her fire red hair was swept into a bun and covered with a cap made of the same orange material but had a huge green and blue peacock feather sticking straight out the front.

Large, gaudy jewels adorned the rings on her fingers, and even bigger jewels adorned the thick gold chain hanging around her plump neck.

When she introduced herself as Lady Esmerelda, Willamina was taken aback. The woman's look surprised her. It was most unexpected from her previous experience with others she had hired. But Lady Esmerelda came well recommended from a former friend.

Now Willamina learned that the person was no friend and instead one of her husband's many lovers. Why she held a grudge against her, Willamina had not the faintest of ideas. But that mattered naught now.

The clearly un-medium-like Esmerelda was a phony. And once everyone was there and she started talking nonsense, her eyes rolling back in her head, speaking words that made sense to no one, and then pointing to the guests and speaking in the most demonic voice Willamina had ever heard, her *friends* could not take their leave fast enough.

Since then, she had been labeled a pariah of society. Not once had she ever asked anyone to pay her monies to attend her parties. Whatever coin had been exchanged was done at their own accord, and never to her.

Unfortunately, now they believed she was just trying to take them for their money. As if the mediums were somehow splitting their earnings with her—which they were not. The news they had received from their loved ones from the grave no longer mattered. True messages, mind you, not fake ones.

Nay, all of that was quickly forgotten.

And that was how she now found herself in Edinburgh.

She spotted an empty bench and took a seat, watching the people as they passed, hoping they would not heed her any attention.

"Lady Watson."

She should have known her peace would be short-lived. Standing, she set her glass of champagne down and dropped into a curtsy before assessing the man standing in front of her. Craning her head up, the man was exceptionally tall, but that was where her interest ended. Beady, brown eyes, just a wee bit too close together perused her from her head to her toes, before he dragged his gaze back up and lingered on her cleavage.

Flipping her fan open, she waved it in front of her chest, using it as a barrier to protect herself from his stare.

"Lady Watson," he repeated, his eyes finally meeting hers. "Your cousin said I could find ye here. I hope ye dinna mind the intrusion?"

From this angle she could see the sharp crook in his nose. It appeared that Mr., well, she did not know his name as of yet, but whoever he was appeared to have broken his nose a time or two.

Truly, she was sure she could expect Gil to send an endless stream of *suitors* her way. Whether she wanted him to or not. She had only hoped that he would be more discerning in his choices.

"He said I should introduce myself to ye. Rupert Wingot. I would verra much enjoy a dance later?"

His gaze had wandered back to her breasts while he awaited her answer. It would be rude to deny him the dance, no matter how unpleasant it promised to be. She noted her cousin a few paces away, watching her every move.

"'Twould be lovely." She forced a smile. "Thank ye. If ye will excuse me, I believe I see an old acquaintance."

Rupert bowed and stepped aside, letting her pass. She felt his eyes on her as she walked away in the opposite direction of her cousin, trying not to rush her steps too much. Though really, she only wanted to get out of his presence and the prying eyes of Gil.

She knew no one here aside from Gil, of course. But the fabrication freed her from Rupert's company—for now.

"Miss Watson."

What now? She spun, excuse at the ready, but any words died

on her lips as Lord Primrose called to her.

He took a quick step back in surprise. "I apologize, Miss. Ye appear to be upset. I do hope I am no' the cause of your distress."

Heart rushed to her cheeks. "Nay." She fanned herself in short, quick bursts. The warmth that flooded her body was entirely due to Lord Primrose's proximity and had naught to do with the air temperature.

He leaned close and whispered in her ear, his breath hot against her skin. "Truth be told, Wingot's attention is enough to make even the strongest person upset." His chuckle was deep and rumbled down her spine.

Looking around him, she noticed Wingot watching them suspiciously.

"I may have fibbed a wee bit and told him I spotted an old friend to get away."

"Smart lady."

His smile and praise made her body tingle. She cursed its reaction.

"Mayhap we should move in this direction so as no' to raise his curiosity."

"Aye."

He plucked two glasses of punch from a tray and handed her one.

"Thank ye, my lord." She sipped from the flute as they walked in the opposite direction of Wingot. She much preferred the taste of the punch compared to the champagne she had earlier.

Gil stepped into their path. "Cousin, I see ye've met Lord Primrose." Her cousin dipped his head in greeting at the man at her side.

"Buchanan, 'tis nice to see ye again." The two men shook hands in greeting. "I didna realize that Miss Watson was your cousin."

"Ye mean Lady Watson."

Willamina almost choked on her tongue. Darn Gil for giving

away her secret. Though why she was trying to keep her title a mystery, she could not explain. Doing so served her no purpose.

Lord Primrose's blue eyes, alight with mirth, clashed with hers. "My sincerest apologies. I had no' the faintest idea. I hope ye did no' take insult in my incorrect address."

She shook her head, her tongue heavy as if her mouth were full of mud.

"Well, Primrose, we shall have to meet for a drink and a game soon."

And just like that her cousin led her away from Lord Primrose and the party.

Willamina had to stop herself from looking back at him as they made their way through the crowd and out to their waiting phaeton.

She could only hope she got the chance to see Lord Primrose again.

"YE MUST MARRY by the age of twenty-eight to retain the title of Earl of Rosebery."

As Finlay finished his glass of whisky, the line from his father's will played over and over in his mind. He was running out of time. His birthday fast approached and he was no closer to being married now than he was when his father passed three years ago.

Why ever the man put such a clause in his will, Finlay had no explanation. Both of them knew that Fingal was incompetent to lead the Primrose family into continued prosperity. It was not something said out of spite, but of experience, watching him throughout the years.

They may be twins, identical in appearance, but that is where the similarities ended. Different personalities. Different paths in life. Different morals and ethics.

His brother would be their family's ruin if he were to ever take charge.

He thrummed his fingers against the wooden surface of the desk, playing out a steady staccato rhythm.

"Think, Finlay. *Think.*"

Miss Watson, nay, *Lady* Watson came to mind.

She was beautiful. Well spoken. Strong-willed, and he detected a touch of a sense of humor in their short exchange. But she was also a wee bit mysterious. Why had she not told him she was a lady when she introduced herself? Why keep that a secret?

He wanted to see her again. To know her past.

She could be the wife he was looking for.

Though her cousin, Buchanan, swept her away with great haste when he spotted them speaking.

Mayhap he would call upon her on the morrow. With her beauty, surely there would be a long line of suitors queued at Buckwood Manor.

He would just have to be the first.

Or, have a damn convincing argument as to why she should choose him.

Mind made up, he poured himself another glass of whisky and pushed away from his desk. It had been a long day, and he was ready for it to be over. The house was quiet as he made his way to his room. He could only assume that meant that Fingal was staying at his own home tonight. Rose Hall, the home Fingal and his wife, Yvette, were given on their wedding day, was on the estate's grounds, though far enough away that Finlay didn't really have to bother with them.

Knowing his brother, he more than likely had gotten kicked out of one of the pubs, and after making his way home, was now losing himself in his wife.

Finlay sighed. He could imagine Lady Watson warming his own bed. Her brown hair splayed across the pillow. Her pale cheeks flushed pink. Her soft skin...

He groaned and pushed a hand through his hair as his cock

stirred.

No matter how long the day was, this night was going to be even longer. Images of Lady Watson would be burned into his mind until he got the chance to see her once again.

CHAPTER THREE

"Cousin, I fail to see the urgency in me finding a husband. Canna I just enjoy living for the present being without the added stress of husband-hunting?" Willamina asked Gil the next day after his butler, Domenic, announced several suitors awaiting to meet with them.

She had no interest in speaking with any of them, unless, of course, one of them happened to be Lord Primrose. Inwardly, she hoped he was here, but at the same time, she did not want him to be. Being forced into another marriage was not high on her list of items to achieve.

With the disaster of her first marriage, it was not something that she was eager to repeat.

She plucked at the corners of the toast Cook had prepared, making a crumby mess on her plate.

"Do stop playing with your food, cousin. Ye are a lady for God's sake, not some petulant child. Stop acting like one." Gil said over the rim of his teacup, before turning his attention back to the book he was reading, ignoring her question.

"'Tis easy for ye to say. Ye arena' the one who is being forced into a relationship that ye dinna want. Or need, for that matter."

"Actually," Gil started, setting down his book and crossing his long legs. "If ye want to keep whatever monies and holdings ye inherited from your late husband, ye should want to marry. Lest ye want me to keep it all," he added.

Sputtering, she had the childish urge to throw her toast at

him. "Ye shall no' do such a thing. Ye wouldna dare."

He raised a brown brow as his eyes met hers. "Dare I? Och, indeed I would. I was perfectly happy having the manor to myself, ye ken."

"Then ye should have left me in Inverness. I also was perfectly happy there as well." She crossed her arms and shot him a glare.

Sighing, he leaned back in his chair. "Mayhap, but even ye must admit, your welcome in Inverness was wearing thin. Thanks to your little escapades with the *undead*." His lips puckered as he said undead, as if he had just bit into something sour.

"None of that was through any fault of mine."

"Really?" he asked with disbelief.

"Truly," she spat. "I will have ye know that I had a verra good reputation with the parties I held. The ladies in attendance were all verra happy with the outcome, each and every time."

He cocked his head to the side as he studied her. "Until they werena."

"Oh, phooey!" She threw her napkin onto her plate and pushed back from the table. "Ye are obnoxious. That was no' my fault."

"Och, but cousin, that is where ye are wrong. 'Twas your fault. Ye were the one who hired the loon."

"I obviously didna know she was a loon when I did so."

Gil shrugged, but said nothing more.

"I am going to my room."

"'Tis fine, but be ready to meet with your visitors in an hour. I dinna mind keeping them waiting. It weeds out those that arena serious. But anything longer than that just seems unnecessarily cruel and spiteful. And at this point, ye dinna need anything else tarnishing your reputation."

Fists balled at her sides, she spun and met his eyes with an icy stare. "Ye truly are insufferable," she ground out.

"Mayhap, but I am right."

He picked up his book, effectively dismissing her.

Darn him and her situation. She was acting like a child, and she hated herself for it. She would not be able to accomplish anything if she kept up this countenance. Nay, she would get further with her cousin if she played nicer. Sweeter.

He always did fall for lasses that, to Willamina, seemed overly sweet and quiet in attitude.

Neither of those traits lived in her being. She was headstrong. Independent. She did not need to rely on anyone, except for what society forced upon her. In those instances, she had no choice.

In the hallway, she heard multiple voices in conversation, and she quickly hurried up the stairs to her room, closing the door softly behind her.

She fell upon the bed with a sigh and stared at the ceiling, studying the design on it. Swirls of paisley had been molded into the plaster and it was quite beautiful. Clearly, it was not something her cousin had commissioned. He did not seem the type to partake in such frivolities. He would probably state the monies it would take to commission such a task would be frivolous and unnecessary. More than likely, it was an aunt or uncle a generation or two back.

Her mind wandered to Lord Primrose once again. Had he called upon her today? Nay, she doubted he would. His interest last night was purely to escape the others at the party. And truth be told, she did not even know if he had a wife. Or a fiancée. The topic never came up in their conversations, of course. Why would it?

She pushed herself off the bed and forced herself to walk over to the vanity. A soft knock at the door alerted her to her maid, Joan, that Gil had most likely summoned to help her prepare to meet their guests.

"Come in," Willamina called and Joan opened the door, quietly closing it behind her, before dropping into a curtsy.

"My lady, I was told ye may need some help getting ready for your suitors."

"By my cousin, I presume."

Joan blushed and nodded.

"'Tis all right. Ye give me someone to talk to instead of that bull-headed oaf of a cousin."

Joan bit her lip to keep from giggling.

"Ye can laugh ye ken. I willna tell a soul."

Joan smiled but held back her laugh. "I shall no', my lady. But I will admit the image was comical."

"Well, let us get me ready to face the wolves. Did ye by chance happen to see how many have arrived?" Willamina asked as she sat at the white vanity table.

Joan picked up a brush, and started to work it through Willamina's tresses.

"I canna say for certain, but I believe Domenic answered the door no less than five times." Her blue eyes were bright with glee.

"Five?" Willamina gasped. "I didna realize I had made such a strong impression during my limited time at the party." It was surprising when she'd only spoken to two men other than Gil.

Joan began pinning Willamina's hair up into a bun, taking care to leave some wisps free to gently frame her face.

"From what I have heard, ye did. Ye are the current talk of Edinburgh."

"Och dear. I dinna want that. Isna there someone else they can focus on?"

The maid pushed the final pin in her hair and patted her shoulder. "Dinna fret. I am certain that this will pass. 'Tis just that ye have recently arrived and all the eligible bachelors have taken a fancy to ye." She wrapped a velvet ribbon around the bun. "An event like that will get all the lassies on the husband hunt talking. Ye are competition that they didna expect."

As her cousin kept reminding her, she did need to marry. Her feelings on the matter played no part. If she wanted to retain the money and holdings from her marriage to Gerard, she had no choice. The only way to do so would be to marry. Her assets would then shift to her new husband.

The trick was finding a husband that would allow her to do what she wanted with said assets and not squander them away for his own endeavors.

She didn't need a love match, but she wanted to be respected. Mayhap she could catch the eye of someone who wanted equal companionship and would just let her be.

She sighed. Men were not looking for a wife on paper only. All her problems would be solved if they were.

Willamina bit her lower lip, deep in thought. What if she caught someone's interest too much? He might then decide to look into her past, and if that happened… Well, then he would learn the truth about her and her past. Did she want that? They would think she was a con artist.

"Now, what gown would ye like to wear, my lady?" Joan asked, pulling her from her thoughts. The maid was standing in front of the wardrobe, its doors thrown open to reveal the contents inside. "'Tis a fair day today. Mayhap this lovely jonquil gown?" She held up the dress and Willamina nodded.

"That one will be fine, Joan." The beautiful shade of yellow would accent her dark chestnut hair.

Joan frowned. "Ye dinna seem happy about the choice. We can choose another."

She stood and approached the maid. "Nay, nay, there is naught wrong with your choice. I just dread going downstairs and having to be on display like a prized pig at the county fair."

"I could only wish that five men would appear on my doorstep for the sole purpose of gaining my hand in marriage."

Willamina felt like she had been punched in the gut. "Och, how insensitive of me. I didna mean to sound ungrateful." She clasped Joan's hands and squeezed. "Ye will one day meet the man of your dreams and it will be the best thing in the world. I just know it."

"I do hope that to be the case." She held up the jonquil gown again. "This one then?"

Willamina nodded. "Aye."

Twenty minutes later, she was properly primmed and ready to meet her potential suitors. Lord, even the thought left a sour taste in her mouth. Mayhap she could talk to her cousin again later in the eve and convince him that she did not need to remarry.

But even as the thought entered her mind, she knew it was foolhardy. He no longer wanted the burden of caring for his widowed cousin, and, at this point, she was quite sure that it did not matter who the groom was.

She would no longer be his responsibility and that was all he cared about.

And in all actuality, whether she wanted it or not, she needed a husband. It would be best if she could find one of her choosing so as not to be married off to someone like Gerard, or heaven forbid, someone even worse.

FINLAY SAT UPON the wing backed chair near the fireplace and chatted with Buchanan. Their relationship was not a close one. They knew of each other more in passing than anything else, but of all the men here, Buchanan was the most interesting to talk to, which did not amount to much.

He looked about the parlor at the other four men who had come calling for Lady Watson. He had never seen a sadder lot than those that lounged about the room, some waiting more patiently than others.

Rupert, of course, was here. He kept swiping at his nose after every bite of the cucumber sandwich he had plucked off the tray that was put out for their visit. A most unbecoming trait.

Finlay kept to the tea that was offered, and took a sip every once in a while. Each time, he studied his competition from above the rim of the cup. He wasn't ashamed to say that he believed he had a high chance of being Lady Watson's choice. A surge of pride swelled in his chest at the thought.

After all, there was Lord Graham, who had lost his wife, and was on the prowl for a younger version. But the old sod was pushing sixty, if not over, and Finlay hoped that Gil had more sense than to marry Willamina off to such a dreadful union.

And then there was Baron Battersby, who in the opposite vein of Lord Graham, was much too young. Was he even twenty? What the hell was he doing here? He was not even established yet, other than the title.

Lord Kelly was Finlay's age, and they had gone to Eton together, but their friend group was not the same. The poor man had gravity weighing him down and was just a midge over five foot when he stood at full attention. Finlay doubted he even came up to Lady Watson's shoulders.

He clapped his hands and rubbed his palms together, eager to get this visit underway. Buchanan was being a twit by making them all wait. Finlay was proud to say he was the first one to knock upon Buckwood Manor's door this morn, but since he had been allowed entry and shown to the parlor, it had been naught but a waiting game.

When Buchanan entered the room, he thought Lady Watson would surely be close behind, but here they were thirty minutes later and still no sign of the beauty.

"Are ye purposely making us wait to see if one of us will give up and leave?" he asked casually, while studying his nails, putting on a front of nonchalance.

"Is it working?" Buchanan laughed.

"Obviously no'," he said dryly. "Considering we all remain."

"Determined ye all are. 'Tis impressive, considering."

That piqued Finlay's attention. "Meaning?"

Buchanan shook his head. "It doesna matter. Willamina can make her own decisions when it comes to whoever she finds suits her. I will allow her that one liberty. But she must marry. So take note, Primrose. I would advise ye to take your leave now if ye are no' serious about such a relationship."

"I am no' sure why ye think I would be here otherwise, but your warning is noted."

Finlay's mind wandered to what Buchanan meant by his 'considering' remark. He acted as though there was something wrong with the lass. Who, in his eyes, looked absolutely perfect.

He wondered if it had anything to do with why she didn't introduce herself as a lady upon their first meet.

The sound of a commotion drew his attention to the parlor's doors. Finlay stood, waiting for what he hoped was finally Lady Watson's entrance.

His prayers were answered when the lass swept into the room, capturing all the air in the room, including from his lungs. Yesterday, he had found her beauty beyond compare. Today, whether it be due to not being outside in the heat, or just because she truly was an angel dropped down from heaven to grace the earth, Finlay had never seen such an exquisite woman.

He wanted to approach her. To push and punch his way through the men that crowded around her as soon as she entered, but he held back. From their brief talks, he had noted a streak of independence. The last thing she would want was him fawning over her. So, he held back, his irritation at its near limit watching the other men making fools of themselves.

He supposed that should make him happy. It would disqualify them more than anything else, but he hated the way they descended upon her as if she were prey. Like an antelope being attacked by a lion.

Feeling eyes upon him, he drew his glare away from the men, and his eyes connected with hers and all rational thought left his body.

Lord Graham was trying to get her attention, but she waved him off. And finally, Buchanan stepped in and told the men to give her space.

The smile she blessed him with made his knees want to buckle. He cleared his throat, trying to break the spell she put him under. But he could not. His gaze followed her as the men parted and she moved to sit upon the settee.

A comely young woman who had accompanied Willamina's entry stood off to the side. Lady Watson's maid he presumed. Seeing the lass, Baron Battersby broke from the crowd and wandered off to the girl, his cheeks flushed as they began a conversation. Someone's parents were going to be quite upset with their son when they found out he was visiting Buckwood Manor to hopefully court Lady Watson and instead took a liking to the maid.

But as Finlay watched them, he thought a match between them would suit them both. But who was he to say?

Smartly, Buchanan sat down beside his cousin, preventing the others from doing so.

"Lady Watson," Graham approached. "Thank ye for seeing me today. Might I offer ye this?" He fished around in his jacket pocket and produced a small box. Willamina watched curiously and her eyes widened when she saw the box.

Surely, the chap would not be so forward as to ask for her hand already? And in front of so many other possible suitors. Well, only one possible suitor in Finlay's eyes, but that was his opinion.

Opening the box, Willamina smiled. "'Tis lovely Lord Graham."

He bowed stiffly. "Thank ye. My family owns a typesetting company and I found it fitting to offer ye a custom key from our finest designer. I hope ye enjoy it."

She nodded and handed the box to her cousin. "Thank ye."

He dipped his head in welcome as he stepped aside to allow Kelly to approach while he shot a look of triumph to Finlay.

Finlay gave him a smirk. The man was old enough to be her grandfather for God's sake. Typesetting business or not, he would need a lot more than that to win over Lady Watson. Of that, Finlay was sure.

Still standing back, he watched the exchange between her and

Kelly. She was sitting down and she hardly had to crane her neck to look the man in the eye. However, he too dug around in his pocket and offered her a gift.

What was it with the arriving with gifts? Had he truly missed that was proper etiquette now when trying to woo a lady?

If that were the case, he was undeniably empty-handed.

What was wrong with plain charm and rugged handsomeness?

Once again, polite as can be, Lady Watson accepted the gift with grace. It was almost as if she had been through the process before.

Her eyes settled on his, a dark brown brow lifting in invitation. He took that as his cue and moved forward.

"My lady," he bowed low, his eyes never leaving hers. "I thank ye for seeing me, but I must confess, I have no gift to offer."

Kelly scoffed. Willamina shot him a stern look and the man practically wilted into the corner.

"My lord. I dinna require any gifts. Though the thought is nice," she added. "'Tis no' necessary."

He gave her a warm smile. "Well, since I canna make such an offering, I was hoping that ye would join me for a stroll through the gardens?" He vaguely remembered visiting the gardens at Buckwood at some point in his distant past.

Graham's and Kelly's heads snapped up at the invite, their brows drawn together in irritation. It was not Finlay's fault that they came with gifts and no other plan.

"See, my lord, ye do have something to offer."

He raised a brow in question. "Pardon?"

"Ye offer me your arm for a walk. What better offer than the gift of companionship?"

Well, if that did not have him straightening his cravat.

"Cousin," she turned to Buchanan. "Will ye join us as chaperone or shall I take Joan?"

He looked at Joan, who was still in deep conversation with

Battersby. And then looked at Graham and Kelly. After assessing their angered faces, he decided to let Joan accompany her whilst he dealt with the two men.

Finlay almost felt bad breaking the blossoming couple apart, but not enough to not do so. Battersby shot him a look, but then glanced at Lady Watson and it looked like a sense of dawning washed over the poor lad and he finally realized his mistake.

"Shall we?" Finlay asked, offering his arm.

Lady Watson nodded, and her hand slipped into the crook of his elbow. He could feel the warmth of her hand through the material of his shirt and jacket. A feeling he did not realize he needed, but would long for forevermore.

Once outside, he leaned in close. "I felt like I should perform a duty and save ye from those monsters inside."

She laughed, a soft melodic sound that was pleasing to his ears. He could listen to her laughter all day long.

"My lord, I am certain that I could have handled any situation they may have thrown my way. But I thank ye, nonetheless. Neither of them are very interesting when it comes to Lords Wingot, Graham and Kelly. And Battersby? What was my cousin thinking? He is practically a child."

"I believe he was thinking that ye need to marry, and from my understanding, time is of the essence from what I could gather."

"My cousin said that?"

"Aye. Is there a reason for the..." he let the sentence trail off. How could he delicately ask what sprang to mind without insulting the woman?

She sighed, keeping her eyes straightforward as they continued along the gravel path, tall hedges enveloping them on each side. "I dinna ken why he said such a thing. I am in no rush to marry."

He tilted his head to the side. "Really? That was no' the impression I was given."

She pressed her lips together and he felt her hand ball into a small fist in the crook of his arm. "Contrary to what my cousin has said, I am no' in search of a husband. So, if that is your intention, we can end this now, and both of us may continue on with our days as if this ne'er happened."

He stiffened. She was upset. The prospect of marrying was off-putting to her. It was apparent by the clouds darkening her eyes. The slightest pull of her shoulders.

"I apologize, my lady. I really would like to continue our walk if ye dinna mind?"

She looked back at Joan and then met his eyes and blew out an exasperated breath. "I do need to marry. However, I do no' want to."

CHAPTER FOUR

THERE. SHE HAD said it. Whether that would deter him from whatever Lord Primrose thought he was doing here, she knew naught.

"If ye dinna mind me asking. Why is your cousin so insistent?"

Surely, he knew that she was of marrying age. At this point, she might as well be headed toward spinsterhood. At least that is what he must think, considering her age. He had no idea she was previously married. Really, he knew naught about her.

Maybe if she told him of her past, he would run for the hills.

She took a deep breath and blew it out slowly.

"Mayhap we should sit for a time?"

"Of course." He hurried her over to a stone bench shaded by a large oak tree.

Joan stayed within eyesight, but out of earshot, and Willamina rubbed her hands down the skirt of her gown, the material soft under her fingers.

"I am unsure of what my cousin has told ye. But my past is a storied one. I am no innocent maiden if that is what ye are in search of. If that is the case, ye should leave now."

To Lord Primrose's credit, his expression remained passive. There was no look of condescension. He remained quiet, his eyes set on hers and waited for her to continue.

How much should she tell him? Everything? Something? The bare minimum? She was not sure. Though she appreciated that he was not pressuring her in any way.

"I was married," she blurted out. She did not mean to say it that way, but it just happened, the words slipping from her lips before she could stop them.

His brows lifted slightly in surprise, but he still said naught.

Even with the sun hidden behind the clouds, the air was so hot out here. Willamina did not have her fan with her, so she waved her hands in front of her face to try to cool down.

Lord Primrose's proximity. The impending conversation. It was too much to deal with. What she said to him would surely scare him away.

The thought both saddened her and made her happy.

For one, she did not want this. But for the other, he was incredibly handsome. Strong, tall. Titled, not that she cared for that. She already had hers. But what would it feel like being held in his strong arms?

Divine. That was what it would feel like. A feeling completely unknown to her.

He coughed, and she was sure it was to bring her wandering attention back to them.

A blush crept up her neck and she gave him a small smile. Why was it so hard to speak to him of this subject? Never in her life had she had a hard time speaking her mind.

Lord Primrose did things to her body and mind that made her feel incompetent.

"My husband passed away a few years ago."

His blue eyes darkened and a frown dipped the corners of his mouth. "I am verra sorry to hear that. My condolences on your loss."

She shook her head. "Nay, 'tis all right. Thank ye, though."

"Is that why ye are under your cousin's guardianship?"

"Aye. Nay." She pushed off the bench and continued down the path they had been strolling along earlier. Heavy footsteps crunched the gravel behind her and soon Primrose was matching her strides at her side.

"When my husband passed, our assets' oversight fell to my father. Late last year, he and my mother were killed when their carriage overturned. Since Gil is my only remaining relative, he now controls all my assets."

Primrose nodded. "I can understand that, but why the rush?"

"Honestly, I dinna ken," she shrugged. "I think he doesna care for the added responsibility. We didna really know each other until this happened, and I believe he sees it as an encroachment of his privacy." She threw her hands up in exasperation. "He could have just left me in Inverness. I was perfectly happy there."

"Ah, ye are from Inverness. That explains why I didna recognize ye."

"I am. And I miss it dearly."

Primrose gently took hold of her elbow and maneuvered her around a puddle in the pathway. "If your cousin did not want the responsibility and ye were perfectly happy in Inverness, than why not just assign ye a guardian there? That way, his life here remained uninterrupted."

The reasoning for that was not something she was ready to get into right now. Though Lord Primrose had set her mind at ease by being so amiable to talk to, she felt like she had revealed enough for this day.

"Mayhap that is a tale for another day, my lord," she smiled so he would not take affront at her refusal.

He grinned. "That means ye would like me to call upon ye again?"

She looked at him, confused. "Do ye no' want to go running for the hills?"

He barked out a laugh, the sound echoing in the small stone tunnel they were walking in. "Because ye were formerly married and tragically lost your husband? I hardly see why that should mark ye as if ye have the pox, my dear lady."

FINLAY COULD NOT believe that Lady Watson would think herself disqualified from marrying again just because she had previously been married.

He needed no fair maiden. A virgin was not a requirement for his wife. As a matter of fact a wife with her first experience out of the way and in the past would actually be a welcome thing.

"I am surprised ye are still interested, Lord Primrose. My cousin doesna believe it could be so. Hence the varying ages and traits of the men currently sitting in the parlor awaiting our return."

"Did ye love your husband?" He cursed quietly, the words spilling forth from his mouth before he could stop them. "If ye dinna mind me asking," he quickly added.

"Our marriage was complicated. I will no' speak ill of the dead, but 'twas no' a love match on both sides. Instead it was part of a long-in-place plan of my parents and him. I did grow to love him, but he did no' feel the same."

He could not imagine being forced to marry someone he did not have feelings for. It was a formula for a miserable life. She did not say as much, but he could read between the lines. It was clear as day that she had not been happy.

"And that is why ye dinna want to remarry?"

She nodded, but said naught more.

He was sure there was more to the story, but he had prodded into her history enough for one day.

"'Tis understandable. Bad experiences make us want to avoid any such thing from happening again."

Biting her lip, she stared straight ahead, avoiding his eyes. "I do suppose that is true. While I dinna want a husband, I would like to regain control of what is mine, without my cousin's interference."

A plan began to form in Finlay's mind. He would have to

think on it more, but he was certain in the end, they could both achieve what they desired.

Desired might not be the best word for what he was thinking, for when he thought of desire, the only image in his mind was Willamina Watson. She was undeniably desirable. And whatever her late husband had done to scar her so, he was a bastard for it.

She deserved to be treated like a queen. Put on the highest pedestal and taken care of so she did not have to worry about a thing.

He loosened his cravat, the temperature was beginning to warm up. Mayhap it was time they rejoined the others.

"Shall we return inside?" he asked. "We have been out for some time and I dinna want ye to get overheated."

She let out a long sigh. "I suppose ye are right. But I do dread going back in there."

"Too many prospects?"

A most unladylike laugh erupted from her throat and she slapped her hand over her mouth.

He found her positively amusing.

"I do apologize for that. But, nay, there is absolutely no one waiting inside that are even close to being prospects. If I were even considering marriage, of course," she quickly added. "May I be frank?"

"I would love naught more, my lady."

She smiled, hooking her arm into his. "Lord Graham is impossibly old. Why my cousin would even make him believe he would be considered is beyond me. Lord Wingot is, well, Lord Wingot, and for that I have no interest whatsoever. Lord Kelly is the right age, if I am being honest, and if I were actually looking, but he seems rather pompous to me. A trait I find intolerable. Not to mention his height.

"And that leaves Baron Battersby, the poor lad." She looked over her shoulder at Joan, who still followed at a far enough distance to make them aware of her presence, but not close enough to hear their conversation. "To be fair, I believe he is much better suited to Joan." She giggled and gave his arm a squeeze.

He dipped down close to her ear. "I do believe ye are correct on that. She did appear to be quite smitten with him as well." He patted her hand lightly, and took note that she didn't pull away.

"I did notice that, too."

As they made their way back toward Buckwood Manor, Finlay found himself enjoying their easy conversation mayhap a little too much.

"I was being truthful earlier," he confessed.

Looking up at him, her eyes round, her pink tongue darting out to wet her lips and he wanted naught more than to bend and capture it between his teeth. She must have sensed his train of thought as her cheeks tinged pink.

She broke eye contact and asked, "About what?"

"When I said I would like to call upon ye on the morrow. I meant it."

He watched an array of emotions play across her beautiful face. Aye, there was definitely more to Lady Willamina Watson than she was telling him. He could only assume it was more than just her not wanting to get married again. Something had happened to her.

Who had hurt her? He wanted to know. He would track them down and make them pay. "If I come, will ye see me?"

Seconds ticked by as he waited for an answer. The time seemed like an eternity. He was half expecting for the sun to set and the night sky to bathe them in moonlight.

"I think I would like that," she answered finally.

He held back a cry of triumph, and instead inclined his head to her. "Then I shall do so."

When they entered the parlor, Graham and Wingot were nowhere to be found. Battersby's face lit up at the sight of Joan and he quickly approached her. However, Kelly sat in a chair near the fireplace, whisky in hand, talking to Buchanan.

"Ah, ye have finally returned," Buchanan stated as he stood

and Kelly followed suit.

"Have Lords Graham and Wingot left already?" Willamina asked, not even attempting to hide that she could not care less that they had.

"Aye, something about other matters to attend. I assume ye enjoyed your stroll through the gardens?"

"'Twas lovely." He turned to Willamina. "And now that I have safely returned ye to your cousin, I shall take my leave. Thank ye for allowing me to escort ye for a walk." He bowed and then wanted to drown in the smile she gifted upon him.

"Buchanan, thank ye for welcoming me into your home. We shall have to meet for a drink one day soon." Much like the game Buchanan had mentioned the previous night, Finlay really had no interest in doing such a thing, but he was trying to play nice. Making an enemy out of Buchanan would not serve his burgeoning plan. "Kelly, I am certain I will see ye in the clubs."

"Domenic," Buchanan called, "Please show Lord Primrose out."

The rest of the day would be spent longing for when he could see Willamina again on the morrow. And when he did, he would have a plan in place. It was percolating in his brain, slowly growing into a life of its own. If Willamina accepted, it would solve both of their problems.

He had only arrived at Rosewood Manor thirty minutes prior when the silence of the house was disturbed. "Finlay!"

He groaned at the sound of his brother's voice calling out to him. What could he want, or worse yet, what did he need? More coin to feed his drinking habit, Finlay assumed. His and Yvette's house was paid for, so it couldn't be that.

"In the study!" Finlay called out, settling into his desk chair and waiting for his brother to enter.

Only it was not just his brother that walked through the door. Hell's teeth. Yvette hung on to Fingal, trying to keep herself upright. Both of them were completely drunk. The sour smell of liquor followed them into the room, making Finlay wrinkle his nose.

"Brother," Fingal called, the word drawn out. His arm was draped over Yvette's shoulder now that she was leaning against the wall.

She was close in age to him and Fingal, but before marrying his brother, she hadn't had an easy life. In all their meetings and discussions, it had not been confirmed that she was probably one of the many whores that Fingal had kept employed throughout the city. Finlay did not say that as an insult to his brother's wife. But she was his brother's usual type of woman. No chase. No courting.

Finlay was certain that was how they'd first met.

"I would like ye to meet my wife."

CHAPTER FIVE

Finlay rolled his eyes, astounded by what had just come out of his brother's mouth. How much alcohol had they imbibed? Granted, they hadn't been married long, under two weeks, but surely, his brother hadn't forgotten.

"My wife. Yvette."

"We've met, ye dolt. I attended your wedding."

"'Twas nice to have ye in attendance, my lord," Yvette drawled.

Fingal scoffed. "Ye need no' call him that. We are all family now."

Finlay pinched the bridge of his nose. What was happening? He forced a smile. "Lovely to see ye, Yvette. Fingal. A word, please?"

His brother pulled his wife to his side and planted a sloppy, wet kiss on her cheek.

Trying to keep his composure, Finlay watched the awkward display.

"Anything ye have to say to me can be said in front of Yvette. She is well aware of our sishuashion."

The word he was attempting to say was situation, but he was too deep in his cups to pronounce it properly.

Beside him, Yvette bobbed her head up and down.

Finlay opened his mouth the speak, and then clamped it shut, thinking of how he could delicately tell his brother to get his arse to follow him to another room so they could speak privately.

Apparently, even in her inebriated state, Yvette knew when she needed to take a step back and clumsily ducked out from under Fingal's arm and pushed him toward Finlay. "Go on, love. I shall wait for ye." She waved her hands in the air, essentially shooing him away.

No matter her past history, Finlay applauded her gusto.

"Fine, brother. Let us go to the ssssolar ssssso we can sssssspeak privately," his brother drawled.

Shaking his head, Finlay swept out his arm to indicate he would follow Fingal out the door and down the hall.

In the solar, with the door closed behind them, Finlay spun on his brother. "How much have ye had to drink? Ye stink to high heaven. Why are ye here? 'Tis evident ye've lost your damned mind."

"Those are fighting words, brother. Juss because ye are earl doesna mean I sssssstill willna kick your arsssssee."

Finlay pierced him with a bored stare. Even in his most sober times, his brother had never been able to best him. "In your state, ye arena kicking anything. I dinna ken why ye bothered coming here. Go home. Ye're drunk and impossible to have an actual conversation with."

Fingal scoffed as if he had just been slapped with the biggest insult on earth. "Ye need to bite your tongue and watch how ye are sssspeaking to me."

"And ye need to sober up. Gather your wife and go home. We can talk when ye've your wits about ye."

His brother shrugged. "Ye willna remain earl," he stated quietly.

"Pardon?" What the hell did his brother mean? "Ye dinna ken what ye are talking about."

Fingal shook his head, a sneer plastered on his ruddy face. "Ye've alwaysss thought ye were better than me." He waved his finger in the air. "Ye will sssee." He pushed himself from the chair he had unceremoniously dropped into and approached Finlay on unsteady feet.

He was so close that Finlay could feel his brother's breath, the smell of liquor overwhelming, as Fingal jabbed a finger into his chest. "Watch yourssself, brother. I'm the only married one in this family." He gave Finlay a shove as he backed away toward the door, nearly losing his balance in the process. "Firssst to find a wife. Firssst to the title."

Finlay didn't bother pointing out the obvious that he clearly wasn't first to the title seeing how Finlay held it.

He shook his head and threw his hands up in the air. His brother was impossible. "Ye canna be serious."

Fingal slapped his palm above his heart, the force nearly knocking him off-balance. "I needed a wife before our twenty-eighth birthday and now I have one. The title issss mine." He rocked against the doorframe, a stupid look of triumph on his smug face.

Finlay barked out a laugh. "Ye truly are daft, brother. That is no' what father's will states. 'Tis no' who marries first, ye fool."

His brother's eyes darkened as he tried to process the conversation, but his alcohol-addled brain was not having any of it.

Finlay poked his thumb into his chest. "I, I repeat, I," he thumped his fist into his chest again for emphasis, "need to get married before I turn twenty-eight. If I dinna, then the title of earl goes to ye. 'Tis no' who is first to the altar, ye imbecile. Truly, brother, ye must leave the spirits alone for a while. 'Twill give ye time to clear your head and think straight. And no' make any of these idiotic declarations."

He turned on his heel and left the room. "Go home, brother," he called over his shoulder. He had no more time for his brother's antics. Shaking his head, he could not believe that Fingal thought it was as simple as that.

He always knew that his brother would be the downfall of this family, but this? He did not think his brother would stoop so low as to threaten him, as thin as those threats were. Mayhap it was Yvette's doing.

Whatever it was, it was naught more than another ridiculous

ploy by his brother to take over the Rosebery title. He entered the study. "Ye and Fingal need to return home. I dinna want to see either one of ye until ye've sobered up and can think straight."

She nodded and stood on wobbly legs.

He shook his head. If Fingal spent as much time planning legitimate endeavors as he did bogus ones, he would be a very successful man.

HAVING HAD ENOUGH excitement for the night, he retired to his room.

The morrow would prove to be an interesting day. One that could have massive repercussions for the rest of his life. He needed to think of the best way to approach such a proposal. In both senses of the word.

Would Lady Watson accept either one?

He could only hope.

WILLAMINA HAD SPENT a sleepless night filled with visions of Finlay Primrose running rampant through her mind. Every time she closed her eyes, he was there. His pale blue eyes boring into hers. She swore she could feel his touch. His long fingers caressing her skin. His warm lips brushing across her own, marking a scorching path down her throat, and lower, lower, to the peaks of her breasts.

"Och!" She blew out an exasperated breath. Was this what it was like when two people cared about each other? Was the act of lovemaking pleasant? Her late husband seemed to enjoy his times with his paramours quite a lot.

If the moans of pleasure and sounds of ecstasy escaping his bedchamber were to be believed, then she would say aye.

He had never shown her such tenderness. Nor had he ever cared to lie with her other than their once a month scheduled coupling.

How she hated that the women he brought home seemed to enjoy themselves so much. She was envious of them. For her, the act was mechanical and unpleasant. There were no sweet kisses in the night. Whispered endearments. Passionate caresses. Nay. It was a task. A deed that he needed to complete as part of their marriage pact.

After the first time they had lain together, she would have been perfectly happy if it never happened again. The experience was traumatizing. One that her mother had not prepared her for. At first, she thought that was how it was for everyone. That it was not an act that was supposed to be enjoyed.

But then she heard the other women. He had to be treating them differently. She could not see how they would have such a pleasurable experience with such rough and uncaring treatment.

Willamina had even tried to speak to her mother about it one time, but her mother told her it was uncouth and classless to speak of such things. She needed to do her wifely duty and provide her husband an heir.

A bairn had never manifested, and she could not say she was not happy about that. To bring a wee one in to such a loveless, unfeeling environment was not right. Though she was glad she never became with child, she often wondered what it would have been like to have someone love her unconditionally. To return the love she gave so freely.

She turned under the covers, sinking her head into the soft silken pillow. When she thought about marriage now, all that unpleasantness rushed back to her. Why would she want to submit herself to such cruelty again?

She did not.

Finlay Primrose did not seem the type to be so unfeeling, but when it came to such carnal acts, how could she tell how he would behave? There was a time when Gerard seemed caring. It wasn't until after they married that he'd shown his true self.

It was not something she would open herself up to.

Never again.

For the rest of the night, sleep eluded her. She tossed and turned, trying to get the horror of her first marriage out of her mind, and her delusional emotions of Lord Primrose out of her dreams.

When Joan knocked on her door the next morning, Willamina welcomed the distraction.

"My lady, good morn. How did ye sleep? I have heard ye already have callers waiting."

Willamina groaned and fell back onto the pile of pillows. Today was going to be a long, exhausting day.

"Would it be possible to tell my cousin I have fallen ill and am unable to see anyone?"

"Ye jest, my lady." She pulled the drapes apart and Willamina groaned at the intrusion of light spilling forth from the large window.

"I am no'. I would gladly waste the day away here in bed than be put on display for a bunch of hungry animals that care naught for me as a person. Instead, they just see me as some prize to win. 'Tis infuriating. I remember when I went through this when I was younger. Going through it at my age is just ridiculous."

Joan ignored her prattling and opened the wardrobe doors, sticking her head inside to see what gown she would choose for Willamina today. Joan could dress her in a barley sack for all she cared. As long it kept the men away from her.

The maid poked her head out and smiled at her. "Lord Primrose is waiting as well." Then smirked at Willamina's reaction.

He had really called again today? He said he would yesterday, of course. But she assumed it was just pleasantries once again so as not to offend her. Especially after what she had revealed of her past.

Well, this indeed made the day slightly better. But it still meant she had to go downstairs and face not only him, but the others as well.

She sighed and slumped into the chair at her vanity. "I suppose ye should work your magic, Joan, and make me as presentable as I am capable of."

"My lady, ye are much too harsh on yourself. Ye are beautiful and wanted. The number of men calling prove that."

Willamina laughed. If only that was what the men downstairs cared about. Nay, she was quite sure there were money signs in their eyes. The hope of deeds in their futures. She was just an afterthought.

Joan continued to brush her hair listening silently while Willamina continued to complain.

By the time Joan had made her presentable, Willamina's throat was scratchy from talking too much.

Ten minutes later she walked into the lion's den. She scanned the room until her eyes clashed with Lord Primrose's. He looked positively dashing in his black waistcoat and tan breeches. His hair swept off his forehead in the style that she found most becoming. She had to stop herself from sighing aloud and embarrassing herself.

The corners of his mouth lifted in a soft smile. All the other callers could leave. She had naught interest in anyone else.

Her feelings clashed with what she wanted and what she needed.

On one hand, she longed for Finlay Primrose. She wanted him. *Craved him.* Her body had never known pleasure, but for whatever reason, she felt like if pleasure was to be had, he would be the one to give it to her.

On the other hand, her heart said she could not marry him. She would never put herself in that situation of no escape again. But her mind was constantly reminding her that marriage was exactly what she needed.

"Cousin," Gil approached, a tight smile on his face. "Thank ye for blessing us with your presence finally." The men in the room chuckled. Except for Primrose. He shot her cousin an irritated look and once again she found herself intrigued by the man she should not be wanting.

CHAPTER SIX

WILLAMINA LISTENED TO the introductions with half an ear and, her gaze just briefly meeting with the potential suitor before straying back to clash with Lord Primrose's intense stare.

As he did yesterday, he stayed off to the side, watching all the interactions. Waiting his turn to approach after all the others had made their introductions.

She had boxes and pouches of gifts piled beside her. While she appreciated the gestures, she really had no interest and would find a way to have the items returned to whoever it was that had gifted them to her.

"My lady," Primrose greeted, taking her hand in his and placing a kiss upon her knuckles, his blue eyes never leaving hers, while he let his lips linger just a tad longer than was proper.

She inhaled deeply, trying not to show how much he affected her.

"My lord," she countered. "How verra nice to see ye again." She wanted to say so much more. She wanted to tell him how she had hoped that he would call upon her again. But proper etiquette stopped her from doing so.

He dipped his head, a smile lifting the corners of his mouth. "I fear I canna go a day without calling upon ye." The statement was loud and boastful. Meant for everyone to hear.

And hear they did, indeed.

Mumbling and grumbling erupted through the men gathered

in the parlor.

"Primrose," one of the men called. Willamina would love to say which one, but she could not.

She remembered not one of the names that were introduced to her before Lord Primrose approached her.

"Aye, Jackson. I havena seen ye about recently. Just arrived from your trip overseas I hear."

The man nodded. "I have. But when I heard the lovely Lady Watson was on the marriage market, I had to ensure making the acquaintance."

She blanched at his statement. She'd never felt like such an object to be bought and bartered with.

Lord Primrose frowned. "On the market? Ye talk of the lady as if she were some prized pig at the fair. Have some manners, man."

Willamina clamped her hand on her mouth to stop herself from laughing out loud. It was as if Lord Primrose had entered her mind and read her thoughts. Sir Jackson narrowed his brown eyes at Lord Primrose before mumbling a clipped apology and slinking to the other side of the room.

Catching Primrose's gaze, she dipped her head ever so slightly to thank him for his defense. She longed for everyone to clear the room so they could be alone.

Gil was deep in conversation with someone whose name she also couldn't remember and was completely ignoring her. Joan was off to her right, hanging back so as not to intrude. But Willamina would like naught more for her to do so. These men calling were exhausting. How long would this go on? She would do anything to make it stop.

"Lady Watson," Primrose called loudly once again.

He really was making a show of things for everyone in the room.

"If it pleases ye, I have arranged for an informal picnic for us to share. Everything is set, and just waiting for my direction to place."

He was offering her an escape from this room which she found to be positively claustrophobic. All these men that had been staring at her were now glaring at Primrose, so she enjoyed the brief respite of being the center of attention. That placement had always made her uncomfortable.

"I would verra much enjoy that, my lord."

His wicked smile sent shivers down her spine as he held his hand out for her to accept.

The gasps of the men as they exited the room with Joan following closely behind was the icing on the cake.

The weather was warm, with the sun high in the sky as they walked across the gravel drive and away from the house. Ahead was her cousin's prized fountain. Something he had commissioned from Italy. The white marble was buffed to a shine that glinted under the sun with huge fish forming an arch over a foaming ocean wave. It was not to her taste, but Gil loved it and talked about how he had come into possession of it whenever he could. She had heard him boast about the cost of it on more than one occasion since arriving at Buckwood Manor.

Usually, it sat alone, surrounded by green grass, in the middle of a sectioned off corner of the landscape to prevent anyone from touching it. Gil feared that the oils from people's skin would damage the marble. She didn't think that was possible but remained quiet whenever he mentioned it.

But today, the grass was covered with items for a picnic. On a large blanket, decorated with the light green and yellow colors of the Rosebery tartan, were teacups and saucers, scones, cakes, and fruits.

"'Tis beautiful, my lord." She could count on her hands the times she had been to a picnic—none. Gerard was too busy with his many paramours and his interests did not lie in romantic acts for Willamina. He would have never done such a grand gesture for her.

"I am glad ye approve and I do hope ye enjoy it."

She was speechless. She sat down and he dropped down

across from her.

"How are ye feeling the husband hunt is unfolding?"

Rolling her eyes, she sighed in exasperation and scrunched up her face. "'Tis exhausting. As we have previously discussed I have naught interest. But since I must I have yet to convince Gil to stop this farce." She bit her lip, thinking she may have insulted him. "I mean no offense, my lord."

"None taken." He looked around them. "No one is within hearing distance. I would prefer ye to call me Finlay, if ye dinna mind."

Did she? This was a big step forward. It seemed small, but was it really? Would she call any of the other men dawdling around in the parlor by their first names?

Nay, she would most definitely not.

"If it feels uncomfortable to ye, ne'er mind. But I must confess, I may have nefarious reasons for setting up this picnic and once again getting ye alone from everyone else."

"Oh?" She was intrigued now.

"Aye." A wicked glint brightened his eyes.

"Well, ye now have me interested in your intentions, sir."

"Tea?" At her nod, he poured them each a cup from the bone china teapot.

She added two cubes of sugar and sipped it to test the taste. Pleased with it, she nodded at him to continue.

He cleared his throat, tugging at his cravat as he cocked his head to the side. If she knew him better, she might think he was nervous about whatever he was about to propose.

"Much as ye find yourself being forced to take a husband, I, myself, am in the same predicament. I feel like we may be of benefit to each other."

Her brows shot up at his revelation. "How so?"

He took a sip of tea before continuing. She could not stop herself from watching his throat bob up and down with the action.

"We both need to wed, but neither of us want to. What if we

married one another?"

The tea she was sipping burst from her mouth in the most unladylike manner. She snatched a napkin and dabbed at her mouth, embarrassed for making herself look like a fool, but she could not believe what had just come out of Lord Primrose's mouth. How did marrying solve their need to not get married? "I apologize. That took me unawares. Pardon?"

He chuckled. "I ken it may seem a daft idea, but it would solve problems for both of us. It would take ye off the marriage market. Your cousin would no longer make ye meet callers, nor would they visit ye day after day. And I would make my father a verra happy man—if he were alive to see it."

She shook her head. "I dinna ken what ye are saying. Though I do agree about the daft part. I believe ye have forgotten the part where I stated I dinna want to marry."

"Right, right. We *would* be married, but no' in the conventional sense. And to be clear, ye dinna *want* to marry, but ye *need* to marry."

She began to stand. "I am sorry, Lord Primrose. I dinna know what kind of woman ye think I am, but I refuse to be some, some pretense of a wife that ye push on to the world whilst ye parade a steady stream of mistresses under my nose."

"Pardon? What? Nay," he grabbed her hand and pulled her down to sit near him again. "That is no' at all what I am proposing." His brows drew together. "I would ne'er disrespect ye in such a manner. E'er. Hell, I dinna want any woman, and I have no mistresses."

"Or men," she stated bluntly.

"Excuse me?" He snapped, pushing his hands through his hair, causing the ends to stick up in all directions. He looked positively flustered.

And positively handsome.

"I have no interest in men, I can assure ye."

LADY WILLAMINA WATSON was ridiculously frustrating. And if this conversation were not going the opposite way of how he intended, he would find it most comical. But she was taking everything he said the wrong way. He'd managed to insult her when that was not his intention at all.

"I am apparently daft, because I have naught idea what ye are trying to propose." She jutted her chin out stubbornly. He found it utterly endearing.

He drew in a deep breath and looked out over the lawn. Joan was still far enough away that if they kept their voices down, she would not hear what they were discussing, and she was doing her best to focus on everything but them.

"Ye are no' daft. Dinna e'er say such a thing. I fear I am not conveying myself verra well. This all sounded perfect in my head as I concocted it, but now that I have said it aloud it sounds positively outlandish. Please, do give me another chance to explain."

He held his breath as he watched an array of emotions play across her beautiful face. She looked back toward Joan before turning her dark blue-eyed gaze on him once again.

She shrugged. "I really am unsure of what ye are trying to accomplish with this conversation." She ran her hands over her pale-yellow gown, smoothing the silk. "But, whate'er 'tis, I shall listen." She straightened her shoulders and folded her hands on her lap and waited for him to continue.

"As a way for us to end our current predicaments, I am proposing that we wed. We could easily convince society that we are a love match. I have no doubt in that."

Her eyes narrowed as she studied him. "What is in it for ye? Other than control of my assets?"

"Your assets will remain yours to do with as ye please. I have naught interest in them."

"I am no' sure I believe ye."

"I have my own holdings. My own coin. I have no use for yours. Of course, if ye agree to this, ye would need to move into Rosewood Manor with me. Ye are free to do what ye will with any real estate or coin ye hold from your late husband."

She pushed off the ground and paced in front of the fountain. "I still dinna understand."

"Lady Watson. I enjoy your companionship. Talking to ye is a joy. Ye are funny and quick-witted. Independent and strong. At night, and whene'er I am no' in your presence, I find myself longing for your company. To be frank and mayhap a wee bit forward, I feel we would make a perfect match."

There, he'd said it. Now he only needed to convince her.

She opened her mouth to say something, but he stood, holding up his hand to stop whatever argument she might be thinking up.

"I know ye dinna want to marry. Nor do I. But life has dealt us both a hand we dinna want. Our only way out is a mock marriage, in every sense other than paper. Our union would be recorded and recognized by the crown. Satisfying those surrounding us, forcing us to make a decision with someone we possibly may not want.

"This," he paused, pinching the bridge of his nose as he tried to come up with the right words. "This agreement takes the decision out of others' hands and puts it in our own."

She bit her lower lip, causing it to plump and his heart skipped a beat.

"A marriage of convenience?"

He nodded.

"What wifely duties would ye expect of me?" she asked quietly.

He expected that question. And he refused to force her into anything she did not want. "Any duties are entirely up to ye. I expect naught. 'Tis no' my right."

"'Tis if ye are my husband."

He bobbed his head in understanding. "True. To the outside world, let them think we are living the life of newlyweds. Happy and blissful. In private, when no one is looking—we dinna. 'Tis a secret I will take to my grave."

Her pause told him more than her words ever could. She was thinking about it. He wanted to throw a fist in the air and claim triumph, but he could not do that. Not yet.

"But ye dinna e'en ken my past?" she mumbled.

"I ken ye were married. Ye are a widow. Your parents have passed. Anything else there is to ken, ye can tell me when ye feel the time is right."

Wringing her hands, she looked from him to the window of the parlor, where the men inside were no doubt growing irritated that they had spent so much time outside. Their anger was not aimed at her. Though he was certain he had made enemies of the lot.

"Why would ye want to be saddled down with me?" she asked, her voice barely above a whisper.

"My lady, ye are beautiful. Saddled down is hardly the phrase I would use. I would be the luckiest man alive."

"Even if the marriage is no' consummated? I canna give ye what ye want. What ye need. What ye deserve in a wife."

He did his best to mask his disappointment. He considered that might be a sticking point and right now he did not care. Just knowing that he would spend the rest of his days with this incomparable woman by his side, brought a smile to his face. "E'en so. If friendship is what ye want, 'tis what I will give ye." That admission pained him, but it was true.

"Aye."

One single word. But it was enough. He did not need more. "My lady, I believe we will have some planning in our near future on how we shall convince everyone we are a love match. But for now, I think we should return inside and request a private audience with your cousin. What say ye? Shall we tell all those rabid men awaiting ye that they shall take their leave?"

She smiled. A genuine smile that lit up her face and chased the clouds from her eyes. He got the feeling that Willamina Watson had not had the happiest life until now. He vowed that though their marriage was on paper only, he would do everything in his power to ensure her happiness.

He could not believe he was thinking the thoughts he was. He was excited that she had agreed. He found himself looking forward to the days they would spend together. The realization that he had actually fallen for this woman and that he had managed to convince her to marry him was not lost on him.

He could only hope that in time, their relationship may bloom and blossom into something wonderful.

And mayhap, just mayhap, one day she would see him as more than just an escape.

CHAPTER SEVEN

Did she just really agree to marry Lord Primrose? After saying she would not remarry? Aye, aye she did. His proposal made sense. It did save her from her cousin. And it apparently saved him, but from what, she knew not. Just like he did not know all of her past, nor did she his.

"Wait!" Lord Primrose called before they returned to the house. He leaned in low and whispered in her ear. "Since we have a deal, we must shake on it."

He spoke so close to her ear that his warm breath sent goosebumps across her skin. She straightened, trying not to show the effect he had on her, and nodded. "I do believe ye are correct, my lord." She stuck her hand out, and Lord Primrose looked as if he was a bit shocked that she agreed to the gesture.

He clasped her hand and pulled her ever so closer. "Soon, ye will be calling me Finlay, *my lady*." He smirked as they shook hands to seal their deal.

Och, Finlay Primrose was going to be hard to resist. But she refused to suffer another marriage similar to her first. She would not be made a fool of.

Not ever again.

Entering into a false marriage saved her assets, and her heart. For the offer, she would be forever grateful to Finlay Primrose.

When they entered the parlor, the other men began to crowd around her, and she shrank back. She really just wanted them all to take their leave.

"Buchanan," Finlay called. "May I have a word?"

Gil nodded.

"In private."

"We can go to my study if that will suffice?"

"'Twill." He turned to her and must have seen the look of distress on her face. "Joan. I do believe Lady Watson may have overheated in the sun. Mayhap ye can bring her to her room to recover?"

If Finlay Primrose was always going to be this thoughtful and kind taking her needs into consideration, it may not be so hard to fake their relationship. She mouthed her thanks to him and she curtsied to the waiting men and left the room, Joan close on her heels, ignoring their mumbles of annoyance.

She cared not. Once again, she hoped they would all leave.

"My lady," Joan said once they were back in Willamina's room with the door shut behind them. "Ye appear fine to me. Is there something ye need?"

Willamina laughed. "Nay, Joan. Thank ye. 'Twas just a ploy by Lord Primrose to get me out and away from that den of wolves."

Her maid sighed. "I do wish Sir Battersby returned. I verra much enjoyed speaking with him."

Willamina gave her a knowing smile. "I could see that." She moved to the small sofa that was set near the window overlooking the gardens and patted the seat beside her. "Come sit and tell me all about him."

Joan flushed, unsure if she should or not.

"Joan, while I appreciate all of your help and service, it doesna mean that we canna have any conversations on other topics. Now come."

Reluctantly, her maid dropped down beside her. "I know he was here to call upon ye, so I mean no disrespect."

"Pfft!" Willamina waved her hand in dismissal. "Absolutely none taken, Joan. Sir Battersby, as sweet as he seemed, would ne'er make a good match for me. He is much too young. But," she said conspiratorially, "he did appear to be rather smitten with ye."

Joan's already pink cheeks turned a deep red. "It canna be, but I enjoyed our conversation. And he is verra handsome," she added.

"He is, isna he? Mayhap we can invite him over for dinner one evening."

Joan shook her head. "Oh, I dinna believe that is a good idea, my lady. He was telling me he has a duty to find a wife."

"Aye," Willamina prodded.

"Well, as ye know, my lady, he is a baron. I am a maid. 'Tis no' meant to be. But I will forever treasure our talk."

"I would ne'er rule anything out, Joan. Sometimes things happen and take us by surprise. A match between ye both is not entirely out of the realm of possibility."

Joan stood, ready to dismiss herself. "I thank ye for your kind words, my lady. E'en if things are not meant to happen, the hope of a dream is always something to cling to." She curtsied. "I will return to get ye dressed for dinner this eve."

Willamina stood and went to the window, not the one that overlooked the garden, but the one that overlooked the gravel drive.

One by one, she watched as her callers left Buckwood Manor, thankfully for the last time. Or at least the last time that they would be here to call on her. As long as her cousin accepted Lord Primrose's request to marry her. She worried her lip between her teeth. What if Gil denied the request? She refused to believe that was a possibility. Lord Primrose was a very good match. Her cousin would see that and agree.

She could then leave this place. Would she be back in Inverness? Nay, but to be out from the watchful eye of Gil would be present enough. And he would no longer have any say about her assets. Something that made her happy. Because she had no doubt if she dragged her feet finding a husband, he would take control of everything that rightfully belonged to her and hide her away somewhere.

She couldn't let that happen. She had no choice. Lord Primrose was truly her salvation.

After the things that life had forced onto her, she did not really believe in fate.

But bumping into Lord Finlay Primrose at the maze at the garden party of Sir Forthington could have been naught but fate.

So she would accept it as such and move on.

Now she just waited for Gil to come talk to her. Knowing that she would have to convince him that she was in love with Lord Primrose after only a few days. Especially after stating repeatedly that she did not want to marry. It was a large task, but she was certain she could make it believable.

After all, she had lied her way through her first marriage and everybody believed she and Gerard were a match.

Ofttimes, people only saw what they wanted to. And when it came to her and Gerard's marriage, there were no better liars than she and her late husband. To the outside world, they were the happiest of couples.

But behind closed doors, it was naught but hell for Willamina. Gerard was happy as could be, of course. Everything played out exactly as he wanted it. As if the world was an orchestra and he was its maestro.

She looked around the room. A place that, if their plan worked, she would escape in the near future. Och, what she would give to be able to listen to the conversation currently happening between Gil and Primrose.

Needing to escape the confines of her room and to get her mind off of whatever was happening in Gil's study, Willamina made her way to the library. Not overly large, but the room was cozy, with two leather loungers that felt like clouds when you sat upon them. She scanned the shelves, letting her fingertips trail along the leather bindings, searching for something that would hold her interest.

Most of the included works were either military, scientific, or biology. Not her favorite subjects. A smaller case in the corner held books she found far more interesting. She had already read *The History of Tom Jones, a Foundling,* but snagged it anyway. She enjoyed the story and it would hopefully get her mind off of whatever was happening down the hall.

Straining her ears, she tried to hear their voices, but no sound made its way to the library.

She had gotten so lost in her reading, that she didn't hear the two men approach, and jumped when Finlay cleared his throat from the doorway.

"It has been settled. In two weeks' time, ye will become Lady Primrose." Finlay beamed at her after making the announcement.

Her heart jumped to her throat. She was thrilled at the thought that he and Gil had come to an agreement. This was the outcome she needed, whether she wanted to admit it or not.

"Gil and I have agreed that the ceremony will be held at Rosewood Manor." He approached and took her hands in his, squeezing them gently as he pulled her to her feet. With strong arms he enveloped her in a warm hug, burying his face in her hair. "Ye're going to make me the happiest man alive," he whispered near her ear.

She shivered, despite the fact that she knew he was only saying it to convince Gil that their feelings were genuine.

He pulled away and she immediately felt a chill at his absence.

"I shall take my leave. Ye have a wedding to plan." He winked at her and her stomach fluttered. "I mentioned it to Gil, but ye need to ken as well. I am giving ye an open-ended budget to plan whatever ye want for the wedding. Make it as extravagant as ye want. I shall see ye on the morrow."

And with that he was gone, leaving Willamina to try to make heads or tails of all the different emotions she was feeling.

"I DINNA BELIEVE ye are getting married. Especially after showing no interest in doing so," Fingal complained two days later.

Finlay listened as his brother ranted on and on. He had been whining about it ever since Finlay had told him the news.

"Brother, your obsession about my upcoming nuptials is fringing on unhealthy. Get a grip, man."

His brother was stalking from one side of the room to the other. If he kept it up, Finlay fully expected to see a clear path being worn into the oriental rug that decorated the middle of the room.

"Ye are doing this just so ye can keep your title."

"Aye. That is quite obvious. I am not sure what ye are getting at."

"Ye dinna love her."

Finlay shrugged. "Mayhap aye, mayhap nay. Love was no' a prerequisite of the will." The last thing he was going to do was tell his brother his true feelings for Willamina. His pull of attraction every time he thought of her could not be denied. But not only could he not admit that to his brother, he could not confess it to Willamina. She had made clear her disinterest in a true marriage.

He was under the assumption her previous marriage was a horrid affair. So much so that she feared another marriage. He did not want her to fear him. If giving her her space and distance was what she wanted, it was the least he could do for her.

Finlay Primrose was a patient man when it came to things he wanted. He was used to waiting until his target came in to sight.

Not that he saw Willamina as a target. Nor prey. But he was willing to wait for her. He would show her that whatever her first marriage was, one between them would be completely different.

"I am so sick of ye getting e'erything handed to ye on a silver platter. As if, as if ye are some damned golden child."

"Really? Ye think that to be the truth? Ye have naught idea the responsibility that lies upon my shoulders," Finlay spat, tired of his brother's childish behavior. Ye spend your days drinking without a care in the damn world. 'Tis time ye grow up."

Fingal sputtered, but remained speechless as he stomped out of the room.

Sighing, Finlay shook his head. His brother had always been coddled. No one had really expected him to ever take over the title and all its responsibilities.

He poured himself a dram of whisky and sank into an upholstered chair set by the massive fireplace. Mayhap Fingal and Yvette would find living on the estate unbearable once Willamina moved in and they would leave to settle into one of the other Rosebery estates far away from here.

Ah, Willamina. Here. In his home. He could not get the vision of her out of his mind. As obsessed with him getting married as Fingal was, he had to say he had the same obsession with his future wife.

The talk with her cousin was simple enough. He stated his intentions. Gil was nonchalant about the whole situation, he was just happy to not have the responsibility anymore. It just proved to him that her cousin really had no interest in what was best for her whatsoever. He was certain that if Kelly, Jackson, Graham, or Wingot had taken him aside and said they wanted to marry her, Gil would have reacted in the same way.

If his memory served him correctly, they had only come to know each other shortly after her parents' deaths and it showed.

That would make sense considering their relationship was tepid at best. Finlay found her positively delightful. In his mind, he saw the whole situation as Gil's loss.

And definitely his gain.

Later, he and Willamina were due to promenade. A proper date that they had been partaking in for the past two days, and news had been spreading like wildfire of their impending nuptials. He had sent word to his best friends and hoped that they would all be able to stay and visit for some time before the ceremony, but the timeline was tight. The last time they were together was when Alexander and Clarissa had married. It seemed so long ago.

They had kept up to date with each other's affairs by letter.

He laughed out loud. He found it comical how it seemed that most of the time when he and his friends gathered lately, it was because one of them was getting married. He was third. Two more to go.

He could see Malcolm marrying, but Gunn? Nay, he could not see that man settling down. He owned a popular pub and inn, The Stag & Dove, in Banchory, and he had a steady stream of women to warm his bed. The thought of that man settling down with one woman did not seem plausible.

The front door slammed, and he sighed. His brother wouldn't take to him for the rest of the day, mayhap longer seeing the way his temper was flaring. That was fine with Finlay. Distance from Fingal was something he always enjoyed.

For being twins, they had never been close. Even when they were young lads. Finlay had always been responsible, while Fingal had always been wild and carefree. The luxury of being the second-born and youngest, if only by six minutes. His status allowed him to sow his oats.

He would not always have the Rosewood estate to fall back on. Eventually, he would need to settle into his own. With his own occupation. He and Yvette would have their own family. Their own estate.

Finlay could only look forward to that day.

He finished his whisky and set the glass on the mahogany side table. He needed to get up and prepare to call on Willamina. One thing he had noted since they had decided to announce their engagement was he had certainly made some enemies. The hard looks he got when he was out and about were uncalled for.

It was not like he had stolen Willamina away from these men. If they had been more charming they may as well have been in this position instead of him.

That everyone believed that they were truly in love just proved that their farce was believable. They had had their doubts, apparently for no reason.

After freshening up, he climbed into his waiting carriage and made his way to Buckwood Manor. Domenic opened the door as he lifted his hand to knock.

"Good afternoon, my lord. Lady Watson will be down shortly and has asked that ye be shown to the parlor to wait. Shall I bring ye a drink?"

"Nay, thank ye, Domenic. I shall wait in the parlor as instructed." He gave the Buchanan butler a smile and walked down the hall and entered the parlor, surprised that Gil occupied one of the chairs. "Buchanan," he dipped his head in greeting.

"Primrose. I am certain Willamina will be down momentarily. I have found that she enjoys making people wait on her."

Finlay pursed his lips, his eyes narrowing. "I think ye mayhap are being a wee harsh with her. The perfect woman is always worth waiting on."

Gil barked out a laugh and slapped his knee. "Well, if that is what ye believe, ye have found the right one for ye. Ye will spend more time waiting than actually doing whatever was planned."

"Cousin, telling tall tales again, are ye?"

Finlay jumped up at the sound of Willamina's voice and spun toward the door, bowing low in greeting. Their eyes met, hers glittery with mirth as she teased Gil.

Finlay let his eyes roam over Willamina. Her green gown fit her flawlessly, the color a lovely match to her skin tone. Cinched at the waist with a wide tartan ribbon. The bodice cut just low enough to tease him with the slightest swell of her breasts.

She caught him looking, and he smiled sheepishly. Not embarrassed to show her she had his full attention. His cock jerked in his trousers and he tried to ignore it. He did not need to scare her away. Though the thought of such a display scaring Willamina away seemed implausible. She did not strike him as someone to be easily frightened.

"Well, cousin, if ye are finished with insulting my character, Lord Primrose and I will take our leave. Who is to be our chaperone today?"

Finlay looked around, expecting Joan to be waiting, but she was not there.

"Joan has other obligations today," she leaned close and whispered, a twinkle in her eye.

An annoyed look on his face, Gil stood. "I get the delight and pleasure to follow the two of ye around this afternoon."

Willamina smiled. "Just think. Ye willna have to do so much longer. I am quite certain that all of Edinburgh is aware of our plans by now."

"Let us hope." He approached them, the smile on his face not quite reaching his eyes. "Shall we?"

CHAPTER EIGHT

O UTSIDE, THE SUN shone bright in the sky, but the air still held a chill. Willamina was glad that she had opted to cover her shoulders with her cloak before leaving Buckwood Manor. She looked back to see Gil far behind them, talking to a man she recognized, but could not remember the name of. He had been to visit her cousin previously.

Her hand was settled in the crook of Finlay's elbow, and she could not help but caress her fingers over the sleeve of his wool coat.

"Lord Primrose, I do believe that we have society properly fooled," she said, dipping her head and smiling at a couple that walked past them.

"I must agree. I had no' thought myself for an actor, but mayhap I should change professions."

She giggled. "I would verra much like to see ye on stage. I would be front row of the theater for every show."

He looked down at her, his eyes crinkled as she jested. "Would ye now?" He shook his head as they walked on. "Nay, I dinna think I could."

"Why no'?" she asked.

His eyes took on a faraway look as he thought on something, but as she waited, he did not expand on his thoughts. She really would be there to watch every show he acted in. It would be a marvelous performance, she was sure.

"I just think my talents would be better suited elsewhere," he said breaking into her thoughts. "I do have something I think we should discuss," he whispered conspiratorially.

She looked over her shoulder, ensuring Gil was still occupied with other things. Satisfied that he was, she focused her attention back on Lord Primrose. "Go on," she urged.

He patted her hand resting on his arm. "Since we are to be married—"

"On paper only," she cut in.

"Of course. But in any case, I feel it only proper that ye address me as Finlay. It doesna make sense to continue to call me Lord Primrose. Or I to call ye Lady Watson. Surely, that is no' how our conversations will go."

She nodded in agreement. He made a good point. They very well could not continue to be so proper if they were to be married.

"So ye should call me Willamina and I shall call ye Finlay?" She could feel the heat rush to her face from the suggestion. Really. She was acting as if she were a lass experiencing her first introduction into society.

"Aye, or a nickname. I would quite like to call ye Mina. It has a nice ring to it. 'Tis just one more way to show that we are in, in, in… Well, ye ken what I am trying to say."

Could he not say the word 'love'? She ducked her head and hid her smile. She found his reluctance endearing and his choice of a nickname for her even more so.

"Well, Finlay," she said the name slowly. It felt odd, as if she were doing something forbidden. But, as he said, with them to be married, calling each other by their formal names would only raise suspicion. And neither of them wanted that. Mayhap she could call him Fin. Mayhap in the future. She wasn't sure she was ready for that yet. "It seems the city is abuzz with our upcoming wedding. I read about us in the society papers this morning," she said, focusing on the task at hand.

"I am no' certain I dare ask, but what are people saying?"

"That we are the match of the Edinburgh season. Which I

find verra odd."

"How so? Because we are lying?"

"Nay. I believe we are both verra convincing deceivers." She found that funny. She'd never been one able to lie, barring the front she'd put on with Gerard. That was different, she was playing the part of wife and doing it convincingly. Was this the same? She was once again playing the part of wife, but this time it felt natural. Mayhap it was because she needed this to happen. Or mayhap it was because feelings were forming that she wasn't ready to acknowledge.

She thought back to the conversation at hand and chuckled. "With me being a widow remarrying. 'Tis no' my first time on the marriage market and I really should be old news that no one has any interest in. But it seems the opposite, and I find that quite odd."

Finlay shrugged. "Mayhap they realize what a lovely women ye are and canna help but talk about ye."

She shook her head. "Nay, I dinna think that is it at all. I believe, mayhap, that 'tis more so *who* I am marrying." She nudged him with her shoulder. "I have managed to catch the eye of one of society's most eligible bachelors. One that many a mother was clamoring to get their daughter in front of in hopes of catching the earl's eye."

"Ye flatter me, Mina. I think mayhap the gossip mongers are having a few slow days and just need to write about something to sell their papers. Tomorrow, someone will come along, or something will happen, and we will be forgotten."

They had made four loops around the square. Seen a number of men and women, couples, families. Some smiled, while others glared.

The women were the worst. The looks they hurled at Willamina she could easily ignore, but if she were younger and this was her first courtship, she would likely have a tougher time brushing off their attitudes.

"We should start thinking about dates. I ken we mentioned

two weeks' time, but we need to settle on the exact date."

She nodded. "Gil would verra much like that, considering his push. He is the only family of mine that will be in attendance, so I dinna need to wait for any guests to arrive. But ye do. What of your family?"

He shrugged, his broad shoulders straining the stitching of his greatcoat. "'Tis just my brother. However, I have sent word to my best friends that I am to be married and would like them in attendance. I am certain that they will appear within the next sennight. Once they are here, any day is fine with me."

"Ye and your friends are close?"

"Aye, verra."

"Do they know what we are doing?" she whispered.

"Absolutely no'. I have told them naught other than I have met the woman of my dreams and proposed."

His eyes clashed with hers, the ice blue bright and fierce. If she did not know any better, she would think he was divulging his truth to her. But this was just a game.

She lowered her voice to ensure no one would hear what she was about to say. "Since none of this is real, what type of ceremony are ye expecting? An actual church wedding with me in a wedding gown? Or Gretna Green?"

His brows furrowed and he actually looked offended at her question. "I only plan on marrying once, Willamina. We will pull out all the bells and whistles and make this the grandest wedding that this city has seen in years. That's why there is no limit on the budget."

She opened her mouth in surprise, not able to come up with anything to say to that. Whilst she admired how he was willing to make this an extravagant event to ensure the city thought their union was real, she did not want to be the one to saddle him down. To stop him from finding true love in the future. He deserved better than that.

Better than her.

"I dinna think that is necessary. 'Tis kind of ye to say this is the only time ye will wed, but we both ken that is no' true. Once all of this blows o'er and my cousin is satisfied, and all the well-meaning, if pushy, mothers leave ye alone, we can have the marriage annulled. 'Twill be entirely possible since we willna have consummated the union."

His eyes darkened and a flash of emotion crossed his face before he replaced it with a smile. Was that sadness?

She was confused at his reaction.

"Let us no' fash about that for now. There will be plenty of time for plotting later."

She placed her hand on his chest. Warmth pooled in her palm. She wet her lips at the touch, then bit her lip and tried to clear her head from the thoughts that were running rampant in her mind.

Glorious, lustful thoughts. But thoughts she should not be having. No matter that he was going to be her husband.

"I dinna want to be the one to stand in your way from finding your true love match, Finlay. Ye canna do that with me and ye being connected forever. When the time comes, we will ken. And we will put an end to our union. Ye can e'en say 'tis me. I willna mind. I can handle another scandal."

"I will do no such thing, Willamina. Hear me when I say, I will take my vows to ye verra seriously. We will discuss this later, away from prying eyes and ears."

They continued walking, remaining silent.

Because really, what could she say to such a statement?

"Come to Rosewood Manor for dinner this eve. Ye can bring Gil, if ye must. Joan is welcome as well." They were nearing the end of their walk and Finlay was not ready to let Willamina go yet—at least not without guaranteeing their next meet-up.

Her eyes searched his. Mayhap she was trying to determine if he was being sincere. Indeed he was.

"We should discuss getting the plans underway. And ye can verify with your cousin what dates work for him."

Willamina laughed. "I can guarantee ye, Gil willna put up any resistance to whatever day is chosen—unless 'tis too far in the future. Then he may have something to complain about."

"I fear ye give your cousin too little credit."

She stopped walking to cross her arms over her ample bosom and cocked her head at him. "Do ye now? Have ye no' talked to him of late?" She rolled her eyes and waved her hand dismissively in the air. "He canna wait for me to be out of Buckwood Manor. It doesna matter now, really, does it? I have no doubt that he will accept whatever date we choose, as I said before. As long as 'tis sooner rather than later."

Laughter bubbled up inside of him at Willamina's wee rant. "I guess we shall find out. Tonight at dinner. Promise me ye will come."

They began to walk again and she made a show of mulling the invite over. "I dinna ken. Mayhap another suitor with his own proposal will come knocking on Buckwood Manor's door and I will be forced to entertain him," she said slyly, a smirk lifting the corners of her pretty mouth. A mouth he wanted nothing more to do than capture with his own. If they were not in the middle of the street and Gil some paces behind them, he might have done just that. To taste her sweet lips. The urge consumed him.

He growled. "Ye wouldna dare."

"Oh?" Her brow raised in challenge. "Do ye no' think so?"

"Ye naughty minx. Ye tease me so. Whatever shall I do with ye?"

"I know naught. But ye will have plenty of time to think of such things once we are wed."

He groaned. Aloud. He could not help it. The things she was doing to him that she did not even realize.

By the time they were wed, his body would be wound so tight, he doubted it would ever unfurl.

Willamina looked at him, innocence dripping from her beautiful face and he knew she was well aware the reaction she elicited from him. And by the look of her face, she was quite proud of herself at that.

While they waited by the carriage for Gil to catch up to them, Finlay did not trust himself to speak. The thoughts that had overtaken his mind were far from proper. And for what he knew would not be the last time, he asked himself if he really knew what he was doing.

The truth was, he did not. Having Willamina live in his house, in such close proximity, and not be able to touch her? He was signing himself up for some self-torture. He only hoped he would survive such a feat.

"Ye look deep in thought. Is something weighing on your mind?" Willamina asked, her hand lightly resting on his arm.

He shook his head. "Nay. 'Tis naught."

Gil clapped him on the back as he finally joined them. "Are ye ready to return home, cousin?" He asked Willamina.

"Aye. Lord Primrose has invited us over to dinner tonight."

"Has he?"

"Actually, I asked Willamina to dinner, but I also extended the invitation to whoever else would like to join—or need to join as her chaperone."

"I am sure we will both attend. I thank ye for the invite."

Finlay nodded. "I thought we could discuss plans for the wedding."

Gil studied Willamina's reaction, and when she nodded her approval, he agreed. "What time shall we arrive?"

CHAPTER NINE

COOK WAS NOT overly thrilled with Finlay's lastminute announcement that they would be having guests join them for dinner.

After apologizing profusely and making amends, she finally gave in and set to work getting everything in order. He had not planned to ask Willamina to join him this night, but he found himself longing for her every moment they were apart.

He was like a lovesick puppy. It was a good thing his friends had not arrived yet. They would jab him relentlessly on his feelings.

Fingal and Yvette walked in shortly after Finlay arrived home. His brother frowned at all the commotion. "Since when are ye hosting dinner parties?" he asked. "Usually, ye just want to sit in your study by yourself being miserable."

"I am engaged now, brother. We need to start planning the wedding."

His brother rolled his eyes and snorted. "Whatever this is," he moved his hands around in circles in front of him. "This whole situation, I am no' believing it for one second. Anyone else, I could. But ye, ye who was so insistent about no' marrying. Now ye are head over heels for the new lass in town? Bollocks."

"Believe what ye will, brother. It matters naught. However, I do expect ye to be respectful to my bride to be and her family when they arrive shortly."

"Och, dinna fash, brother." He snapped his heels together and straightened his shoulders as if falling into formation for his captain. "I will be on my utmost best behavior."

His devilish smile did not set Finlay's mind at ease and as he watched Fingal leave the room, he wondered if his brother had some tricks up his sleeve. He seemed far too excited about their impending company.

Yvette remained behind, wringing her hands together, looking like she wanted to say something.

"What is it, Yvette?" he asked impatiently.

Her gaze drifted to the door Fingal had disappeared through. She opened her mouth to speak, but snapped it shut. Shaking her head, she hurried after her husband.

There was no time to dwell over what Yvette might or might not have said. Willamina would be arriving soon and he needed to make sure everything was perfect.

Looking over the final touches of the table that had been set, Finlay had no idea what he was looking at. Was the setting correct? He would assume so. He had never set the table in his life. And it was not like he could ask Fingal, nor would he. He feared his brother would know even less than he did. Mayhap Yvette would know, but he didn't want to ask her either.

"A carriage approaches, my lord." Archibald stated from his perch at the window. His butler had been like a hawk stalking his prey as he waited for a glimpse of their company. If Finlay didn't know any better he would think that his butler was almost more excited than he was.

"Show them in, Archibald."

Finlay's palms were sweaty and he wiped them on his trousers. His nerves were at high peak, which made no sense to him. He had served in the war for God's sake and had never had this type of reaction.

Time seemed to slow and drag as he waited for Willamina to enter Rosewood Manor. He hoped that she liked the estate. He was anxious to show her every nook and cranny of Rosebery lands.

He was standing near the door when Archibald swung it open and greeted Willamina and Gil.

Finlay's breath hitched. Willamina was dressed in a periwinkle gown with capped shoulders and an empire waist. Her hair was piled on the top of her head in a mountain of curls, with a wavy tendril hanging loose on each side. At her throat, a gold chain adorned with a golden capped silver acorn, hung delicately.

He took her hand and placed a soft kiss on her knuckles. "Ye look beautiful, Willamina."

Her cheeks flushed pink and she dipped into a curtsy.

"Thank ye, Finlay. Ye look quite dashing yourself."

He puffed his chest out at her compliment. He had never much cared for such accolades, but when they came from Willamina, he wanted to hear them all day.

"Buchanan," he greeted, shaking his hand. "Please, let us sit in the parlor for a before dinner drink. Cook has worked hard to provide us a meal fit for a queen and will be serving it shortly."

In the parlor, Finlay poured three glasses of wine and handed Willamina and Gil each one, then held up his own glass. "I think cheers are in order."

Fingal chose that time to burst into the room, Yvette close on his heels. "Dear brother, are ye celebrating without us? Now that is rude, I daresay."

Finlay rolled his eyes.

Willamina's eyes rounded in surprise. Och, in all the times they had talked, he had never brought up his brother, nor the fact that they were twins. Identical at that. Fingal was always at the back of his mind, especially when he was with Willamina. Why waste thoughts and energy on such a louse?

"Fingal, let me pour ye and Yvette a glass and ye can celebrate alongside us."

"Aye. I wouldna miss this celebration for anything." He sneered and accepted the wine Finlay offered.

"Willamina, this is Fingal, my brother, and Yvette, his wife."

She stood and gave him a quick curtsy. "'Tis nice to make

your acquaintance, sir. I had naught idea Finlay had a brother, ne'er mind a twin." She smiled at Yvette. "Nor did I ken he had a sister-in-law. 'Tis verra nice to meet ye."

Fingal laughed. "I am no' surprised. When one is the black sheep of the family, he tends to no' be mentioned in polite company."

"I am certain that is no' the case, Fingal," Willamina said kindly.

"Well, mayhap no'. However, I do agree that a celebration is in order." He held up his glass and the others followed suit. "To my dear brother, congratulations on the win. To his lovely bride to be, Willamina, ye may be a prize, but I do hope he makes ye happy."

Her brows furrowed in confusion, but she held up her glass in salute before taking a sip. Her eyes darted between them. "I am uncertain what ye are referring to, sir, but I thank ye for the salute."

"My lord," Archibald called from the doorway. "Dinner is served in the dining hall."

"Thank ye, Archibald. We will be there momentarily."

Really what he wanted to do was go over to his brother and swat him in the head. Or box his ears. Or beat his arse. He should have known that his brother would spend the night making jabs at him. And by the look on Fingal's face, he knew exactly what he was doing and how annoyed Finlay was.

"Shall we?" Finlay asked Willamina, offering his arm, so he could escort her to the dining hall.

She accepted his arm and let him lead the way out the room. She leaned in close. "I did no' ken ye had a brother."

"Aye," his voice was clipped. "I apologize that he did no' come up in conversation whilst we were talking. I tend to try to push him out of my mind." He pulled out her chair to allow her to sit before dropping in his own chair at the head of the table.

"I have ne'er had any siblings, myself. I would expect that it would be difficult to try to purposely forget them."

A small wave of guilt rushed over him. Her statement made sense—if one did not know his brother. But knowing his brother as he did, her statement was entirely incorrect. She would realize that if she ever got to know Fingal the same way Finlay did. And since his brother was apparently hell-bent on making his feelings of being shorted for the family fortune and title known to all in attendance, he was thinking that she would realize the will of his ways sooner rather than later.

WILLAMINA SIGHED, RUNNING her hand along the wooden banister of the curved staircase as she descended the stairs. She was on her way to meet with Joan in the salon to discuss what needed to be ordered. Honestly, she was fine with a simple ceremony. Low budget and not over the top, but Finlay insisted it be extravagant and that he spare no expense.

Guilt ate her stomach. She felt bad spending any money on what was in essence a farce. He should save his money so that when, in the future, he married for true, he could spend all he wanted. Wringing her hands, she paced the length of the salon, waiting for Joan to arrive.

Willamina missed Inverness. Planning a wedding, fake or not, should be shared with friends. Joan was a sweet lass, and Willamina enjoyed her company, but Joan was here because she had to be, not because she wanted to be.

But even if she were still in Inverness, would her friends really want to help her plan? Nay, she had no more friends. How easily one could turn on another on rumors spread to inflict pain and dissidence. It just proved to her that they were not her friends at all.

"My lady, good morn. Have ye broken your fast?"

"Good morn, Joan. I havena, but I am no' hungry right at this moment." She had met Gil in the dining hall this morn as he broke his fast, but she had no appetite. Anything Cook offered she graciously turned away, assuring the sweet woman that it was only because she wasn't hungry. She patted the seat beside her, inviting Joan to sit next to her.

"This afternoon, I have an appointment with the modiste to discuss gown designs."

"How exciting, my lady," Joan clapped her hands together, a wide smile on her face. "Until then, what shall we do?"

"I need your help planning the guest list. As ye know, with me being new to the city, I do no' ken most of the people here. Mayhap ye can tell me who should be invited?"

"Let me fetch a quill, ink, and paper and we can get started. How exciting!" The maid jumped to her feet and hurried out of the room and returned a few moments later, her cheeks flushed from hurrying to and fro.

Three hours later, Willamina had the list of attendees in hand. Hopefully, Finlay would be happy with them. She really had no idea of the suggestions Joan made. They seemed to make sense when she explained why a particular person should be invited, so Willamina accepted the suggestions and would discuss them with Finlay the next time they were together. Of course, she couldn't speak to who he wanted to have in attendance. She would get his request and give it to Joan to add to the list.

They were less than two weeks away from their wedding now. Her nerves were making her anxious, which made no sense whatsoever. The marriage was not real. They had no feelings for each other.

Even as the thought entered her mind, it left just as quickly.

She bit her lip and thought about the way she felt about Finlay. While she did not have feelings for him as far as love went, he did seem to elicit a certain reaction from her every time he was near. She felt the flush of her cheeks as the images flooded her mind. What would it be like to kiss Finlay Primrose? Certainly he was a better kisser than Gerard. That was hardly a feat.

Gerard's kisses were sloppy and entirely unromantic. How

the louse had a constant stream of women parading through their house, she had naught idea.

Mayhap kisses were supposed to be sloppy. She did not know. Mayhap she would never find out.

"My lady, the carriage awaits to bring ye to the modiste," Joan said excitedly.

"Well, then. I suppose we shouldna leave the coachman waiting, should we?"

"I have ne'er been to the modiste before, my lady. I have always wanted to. Just..." she let the sentence hang in the air unfinished.

"Sweet Joan. I am happy to remedy that for ye today." Joan had been so kind to her. She made a note to talk to the modiste in private and request that she make a gown for Joan. It was unorthodox, she knew. But mayhap one day her maid would find use for it.

The modiste shop was in the center of the city. The tan brick building was three stories high and narrow, with a huge white awning and accents decorating the front. The thick door was made of oak and creaked when Madame Boulet swung it open and welcomed them inside.

The short woman was bright-eyed with plump cheeks and a kind smile. Barely reaching Willamina's shoulders, what the woman lacked in height she made up for with her huge personality.

"Welcome, my lady. I hear that ye are planning a wedding and are in need of a gown." Madame Boulet stood back and assessed Willamina from head to toe.

She blushed from the scrutiny.

"Lord Primrose is a lucky man. Now, would ye care for a cup of tea before we get started?"

Willamina shook her head. "Nay, thank ye." She didn't think her stomach could handle it.

"All right, then." Madame Boulet clapped her hands together and looked about the room. "Where would we start first?"

Willamina shrugged. She really had no idea.

"Do ye have a design in mind?"

Willamina worried her lower lip as she wrung her hands in her lap. She did not, but was she supposed to have? She supposed when women arrived at a modiste for a wedding gown that they had some sort of inkling as to what said dress should look like.

She did not have a clue. Even with her marriage to Gerard she had no say in her wedding gown. It was an abomination that her mother had chosen and it did not fit Willamina's style at all. Not that she was even sure what her style was, but she at least knew that monstrosity was not it.

Seeing her distress, Madame Boulet smiled warmly. "No need to fret, my lady. I have many designs here that ye can review, and if there is something ye dinna see, just let me know. I can customize anything ye want."

"That is verra kind of ye. However, I dinna have a lot of time for such customization."

The modiste dismissed her statement with a wave of her plump hand. "Nonsense. I am aware of your timeline. My schedule has been cleared, thanks to your dear husband to be, so let us get started."

She walked to a wardrobe taller than the one Willamina had in her room at Buckwood Manor and pulled the doors open. She extracted several gowns and brought them over to hang on a high rail set into the wall. "Do any of these catch your eye, my lady? Ye are welcome to come touch them. Dinna be scared."

It was not that Willamina was scared. She was overwhelmed by everything she was being presented with. For her first marriage, she did not have a say in what her gown looked like. It was purchased without her insight and she was told that she would wear it and smile, no matter what.

But, here, she had multiple dresses at her fingertips, and more if she did not find any of these satisfactory. Several shades of white stared back at her. Different materials of satin, silk, lace, everything Willamina could dream of was on display.

One of the gowns seemed to call her name. It was ivory with a satin bodice. A violet lace overlay ran down the middle front all the way through the bodice and skirt to the floor.

"Ah ha. I know that look." Madame Boulet said, pointing a knowing finger at Willamina. "I see your eyes are drawn to this beauty. 'Tis lovely, I admit. Shall we try it on?"

"Now?"

The modiste laughed. "Of course, my lady. How else will ye know if this is your gown or no'? Or how it fits."

A few long moments later, Willamina stood in front of the mirror, the gown accentuating her body in all the right places. The violet played off her skin tone perfectly. Madame Boulet appeared with a lace veil, with violet highlights that matched the design of the lace overlay, and pinned it into her hair.

Willamina could only stare. And for a moment, she wondered if Finlay would like it.

If his breath would catch when he saw her walking down the aisle? Would his pupils darken with desire?

And then she remembered, it was not real.

Even so, she found herself hoping that he would like it. She only wanted to see his expression when she appeared in this dress on their wedding day.

"Ye look beautiful, my lady," Joan whispered. "Lord Primrose will no' be able to take his eyes off ye."

Madame Boulet snapped her fingers. "And that is how ye know 'tis the perfect dress. Ye are the first person I showed this one to. 'Twill be a surprise to e'eryone. Here, let me make some slight adjustments." The modiste set about pinching and pinning. Measuring and marking. "I will have this for ye in a few days. Shall I have it delivered to ye when 'tis ready?"

"That would be verra kind of ye, Madame. If ye could send it to Buckwood Manor, I would be most appreciative."

"Of course, my lady. Before ye go, I have some special pieces to show ye that I think ye may enjoy." She peered around Willamina to look at Joan, and they shared a conspiratorial smile.

"This way."

Willamina followed the woman to another room and her eyes widened. "Oh my," she squeaked. The items here were definitely not for the wedding ceremony, but were fit for the wedding night. Assuming, if the couple was to consummate their marriage, that is.

Madame Boulet laughed. "I have a friend in France that makes the most beautiful negligees you will e'er find. E'ery bride must have at least a few—to keep their honeymoon exciting."

She supposed that must be true of some brides. Mayhap most brides really. Not surprisingly, she did not have any for her first marriage. And for this marriage such extravagances would be a waste. But she could not confess that she would never wear them. Are these truly things that a bride would wear for her husband? Her fingers floated over the soft lace and satin pieces, some looking like it would appear she was barely wearing anything at all.

They were lovely, she had to admit. It would be such a waste of a beautiful piece. But, nonetheless, she picked out four of the seductive outfits and before she could forget, she mentioned her idea from earlier.

"Madame Boulet, do ye think 'tis possible to make a gown for Joan?"

"Your attendant?"

Willamina nodded.

"A most unusual request from a lady, but aye, I could do that if ye wish."

"I do. She has done so much for me, I want to return the favor to her in some way."

Madame Boulet smiled and patted her hand. "'Tis verra kind of ye and I am sure she will be most appreciative. "I will have it delivered to Buckwood Manor with your gown if that pleases ye?"

"That would be wonderful, thank ye."

"I will box these items up for ye. Would ye like to take them with ye today or shall I have them delivered as well?"

Anxious to return home, she opted for the delivery and said her farewell.

On the ride home, the only thing she could think about was wearing one of those negligees and seeing Finlay's eyes flare in appreciation.

Och, she was daft.

Finlay Primrose had no interest in her outside of using her as a way to ward off meddling mothers trying to shove their daughters upon him.

CHAPTER TEN

"MY LORD, DUKE and Duchess Gordon have arrived," Archibald announced as Finlay sat at the desk in his study, mulling over the books containing the estate's finances.

"Ah, great news, Archibald." Finlay clapped him on the shoulder as he stood and pushed past him to make his way to the courtyard.

One of his best friends, Nicholas, was helping his lovely wife, Gwen from the carriage. The footmen were unloading the trunk from the back with Archibald showing them where to carry it.

"Nicholas! Gwen!" Finlay bounded down the steps to meet them. The men shook hands, clapping each other on the back, and Finlay placed a kiss on Gwen's cheek. "I am so glad ye came. Ye look lovely, Gwen. Motherhood suits ye well."

"Hey, ye're getting married, leave my wife alone," Nicholas chuckled. "And we wouldna miss it," he added.

"Hello, wee one," Finlay tickled the brown-haired bairn Gwen held in her arms, eliciting a drool-filled smile from the lad. "Arena ye a handsome fellow?"

"He takes after his father, obviously," Nicholas joked.

Finlay smiled. His friend had come such a long way when it came to dealing with the scars that marred half his face. Before he met Gwen, he was always hiding behind a mask. Now, it was more common to see him sans mask than with it.

"Finlay, I have to say, we were both shocked when we heard the news. But also verra happy for ye." Gwen gave him a warm smile that would melt the heart of even the coldest man.

"Aye, when do we get to meet the poor lass?" Nicholas asked.

Finlay pierced his friend with a look that told him he was not amused.

"Ye ken I jest, brother."

"But we do want to know when we can meet her," Gwen said excitedly.

"Ye both must be exhausted and hungry from the ride. Come on inside and I shall have Cook put something together to hold ye o'er until dinner. Willamina will be here then."

"Och, lovely. I canna wait to meet her. I need to know the woman who won o'er your heart, Finlay. I didna think it would happen. Ye seemed so happy to remain single."

Even his best friends did not know that he had to marry by the time he was twenty-eight. And he was not about to tell them of his and Willamina's plan to get everyone to leave them alone.

"Well, Gwen, when ye meet someone and right away, ye know they are something special, 'tis hard to deny."

Gwen sighed. "How swoonworthy, Finlay. She is a lucky lady."

He felt like he was the lucky one. He just needed to convince Willamina of that. He realized this started as a way for him to keep the busy-body mamas away, but the more time he spent with her, the more he knew he was on the path of no return.

Showing her that they did not need to go their separate ways once all of this blew over was going to be the hard part, considering her stance. There was no clause in his father's will that alluded to a certain length of time for the marriage, but it did not matter. Willamina Watson was wiggling her way into his heart, and he was not about to let her go. Somehow, some way, he would make her see that.

"Have ye heard from the others?" Nicholas asked, drawing his thoughts back to the conversation at hand.

"Aye, they should all arrive shortly. Tomorrow at the latest, I anticipate."

They settled in the salon, and soon Cook brought them finger sandwiches and tea to snack upon.

"'Twill be nice to see e'eryone. It has been far too long since we have all gathered together," Nicholas said.

"Aye, since Alexander's wedding. How are he and Clarissa getting on?" Finlay asked of their friend and his new wife, who was also Nicholas's sister.

"They are well. Ye will see," Gwen said with a secretive smile.

Finlay raised a brow in question. "Am I missing something?"

"Ye shall see." Was all she would say and then bit into the cucumber sandwich she had plucked off the tray.

As the day wore on, his other friends arrived. First, it was Gunn Burnett, Laird of Leys, who owned an inn and pub in Banchory. Then Alexander and Clarissa, the Duke and Duchess of Argyll, who were soon to be parents from the swell of Clarissa's belly. And finally, Malcolm Kennedy, Earl of Cassilis.

By the time Willamina arrived for dinner, Rosewood Manor was a raucous affair.

Introductions were made and before he could blink Gwen and Clarissa had whisked Willamina away. Lord only knew the things they would tell her.

The men had moved into the study, nursing whisky and smoking cigars.

"I canna believe ye made the jump, Finlay," Alexander commented, taking a long pull from his cigar, then making smoke rings as he exhaled.

"And I canna believe ye are going to be a da. Poor Clarissa, how is she going to handle having two children in the house now?"

Laughter erupted in the room, and Alexander took the jab in stride. "She is a saint. Willamina looks like a lovely lass. I do hope my wife and Gwen arena corrupting the poor woman."

"Och, I dinna think we need to fash about that."

Let us hope no'," Nicholas said. "How did the two of ye

meet?"

Finlay chuckled. "A garden party of all places."

A chorus of nays sounded off.

"Ye hate parties," Malcolm said.

"I know. I was guilted into attending this one." A bit of a lie, though he had told Northington he would make an appearance; if it had not been for his father's will, he probably would have found some excuse to not attend. But he could not tell his friends that. They needed to believe this marriage was real. He would in no way bring the slightest inkling of embarrassment to Willamina. Their secret would remain their own.

"Well, I am happy for ye," Gunn announced. "She is lovely and must be one special lass to have caught your interest. Congratulations, brother."

They all held up their glasses and cheered.

"Slainte!" They shouted and downed the rest of their whisky.

Finlay poured them all another round, and they sipped this glass a little slower. There was no need for him to get so deep into his cups tonight that he lost his wits about him, making him say things that should stay private.

His mind wandered to Willamina. He had not seen much of her today, apart from when they sat down to dinner. But before and after then, Clarissa and Gwen had occupied her time. He was sure they were busy discussing whatever women talked about when it came to weddings, but he would be lying if he said he did not miss having her by his side.

A few more days and she would be his. He was eagerly awaiting the time when he could call her wife.

Even if it was not real.

He would make it so.

WILLAMINA WAS OVERWHELMED by the kindness shown to her by

Clarissa and Gwen. They welcomed her with open arms into their friend group and she could not help but feel a wave of guilt every time they talked about how great it would be to add another woman to the group.

Gwen talked about her wee bairn that had settled in for the night.

And Clarissa talked about how she could not wait to give birth and for her bairn to meet her cousin. "Ye know, we must all stick together," she said. "Have ye and Finlay discussed children?"

Willamina nearly choked on the sip of wine she had just taken.

Gwen rushed toward her, patting her on the back.

Once she had her wits about her, she apologized. "So sorry, I fear I swallowed that wrong. But, nay, we have had no such discussion." It was not a lie. They had not. Nor would they. Why for? For a farce of a marriage that they would escape from as soon as it was possible to do so.

Clarissa waddled over, her hands lovingly stroking her rounded stomach. Each time she rubbed her belly, she got a dreamy look in her eyes. "I am certain the conversation will happen soon enough." Being with child suited her well. Her skin positively glowed, her eyes bright.

"Do ye have plans for more children, Gwen?" It felt a bit odd addressing the duchess by her first name, but she had insisted earlier that she wanted to be called Gwen. Clarissa did the same.

They were both lovely women, and if her situation was different, Willamina thought that she would enjoy being friends with both women.

"Both Nicholas and I have fairly large families. Both of us want the same for ourselves."

Clarissa giggled. "Nicholas is going to have to build another wing on the house to accommodate e'eryone."

Being an only child, Willamina had no experience with large families, even when she was married. Gerard was also an only child, so she had no idea how to handle multiple siblings.

"Surely, your family must no' be that big?"

Gwen shrugged. "Well, Nicholas and I, and the wee one. Nicholas has six siblings; obviously, Clarissa no longer lives at Huntly, but the other five still do, along with his mother. Though she spends a lot of time in Edinburgh since we married. I have three younger brothers that also live with us."

Willamina did the quick addition. Ye have 9 children living with ye?" She could not hide the disbelief in her question.

With a laugh, Gwen nodded. "Aye, but most are older. We just have our youngest siblings that we need to worry about. They are forever causing a ruckus."

"And ye wouldna have it any other way, sister," Clarissa quipped.

Gwen rolled her lips, her eyes filled with glee. "'Tis true. I love them all and having them with us brings me joy."

"I am verra happy that ye both have found such happiness in your marriages."

Clarissa waved her hand in the air. "As will ye, Willamina. Finlay really is a caring man. Even if he seems a bit stiff on the outside. Break through that barrier and he will be like putty in your hands."

She caught her lip between her teeth and nodded. Looking out the window so that they could not read her thoughts.

"Finlay is indeed verra kind."

"Ye arena from Edinburgh, I believe I heard Finlay say, aye?"

"Correct, I am from Inverness."

"What brought ye here?" Gwen swatted at Clarissa for her question. "What?" She rolled her eyes. "Ye dinna have to answer if the question makes ye feel uncomfortable. Curiosity got the better of me."

Willamina had no plans to tell them the full story, but she did explain how after the passing of her husband and her parents, her cousin thought it a good idea to come to Edinburgh to find a husband.

Clarissa shook her head. "Leave it to a man to pull ye away

from a place that makes ye happy so he can tell ye what to do."

"Clarissa!" Gwen chided. "Watch your tongue. If Alexander hears ye speaking that way…"

"He will do naught. He loves me. My outspokenness and all."

And that was how the rest of the time spent with Gwen and Clarissa went. They fell into easy conversation, and they teased each other relentlessly as if they truly were siblings. But just looking at them and their interactions together one could tell they loved each other very much.

Willamina, in some odd way, found herself longing for such acceptance. She had never received it from her parents and certainly not from Gerard. Would she ever find herself surrounded by such love?

She could only hope.

CHAPTER ELEVEN

"ARE YE READY?" Finlay asked as he stood in the foyer of Buckwood Manor.

Willamina had just descended the stairs in a beautiful rose-colored gown that made her skin glow. Tonight, he was taking her to the opera. It had been years since he had attended one himself, but he thought she might enjoy it.

With only two days left until they were married, they were spending nearly all of their days together. And the opera he had chosen to see this eve was one of love and longing. Would Willamina sense the hidden message?

He doubted that very much. She had been very businesslike about their whole situation. Sticking to their ruse and calling it naught but that.

For someone who had not wanted to get married, meeting Willamina changed his mind about that quickly, and now it just was not something he *had* to do, it was something he *wanted* to do.

"Ye look beautiful. I fear all eyes may be on ye at the playhouse instead of on the show."

She smiled and put her hand on his arm. Heat seared his skin where her palm rested. "Ye are much too kind."

"I am being honest. Shall we? I dinna want to be late."

He followed her out the door and helped her into the carriage. Gil had decided since they were to be married, they could attend the opera alone. Lord knew there would be plenty of witnesses if things were to go awry.

At the playhouse, they found their way to the box that he held in long reserve. Lots of eyes were on them as they sat and waited for the opera to start.

A few men came over and greeted them. A few women as well, but they mostly let them be to enjoy the show.

The curtains opened and *Orfeo ed Euridice* began. Finlay had seen it before, so he spent the majority of the opera watching Willamina's reactions. Her smiles and her tears. The way she clutched at her necklace when Orfeo once again lost his wife, for what was presumed to be eternity until the God of Love could no longer take Orfeo's mourning, and reunited the pair once again.

Finlay handed Willamina his handkerchief and she gave him a thankful smile as she dabbed at the tears pooling in her eyes.

He loved the way she immersed herself in the show. Her pleasure in watching tugged at his heart.

Two days.

In two days she would be his.

What would happen when everyone left after the ceremony only time would tell. He would not force anything upon her, but he could try to sway her into seeing what he saw.

And that was that they were meant to be.

"This was lovely. Thank ye for bringing me."

"If I had known ye enjoyed the opera so much, I would have taken ye sooner."

She shook her head. "I didna know I did. I have ne'er been," she confessed, her cheeks tinging pink.

Finlay had to hold his tongue from a biting remark about what a louse her late husband was. He did not like to speak ill of the dead, but if anyone deserved to be spoken ill of, he was definitely the one. Seeing how enthralled she was by the performance. Seeing her face light up. Her tears well. How could someone not want his beloved to experience such pleasure?

But she was not his beloved. She had mentioned that before.

"I am sorry your late husband didna treat ye to the theater.

'Tis something ye deserve."

"Ye are verra kind. He wasna one to," she paused as if searching for the right words. "He wasna one to take my feelings into consideration when it came to the arts."

Taking her hand into his, he stroked her gloved hand. Her eyes rounded and darted to the people surrounding them.

"Dinna fash, no one can see. And we are to be married in two days' time. No one will say a word."

She relaxed a little, her shoulders dropping just a bit and she gave him a warm smile.

"And in regards to the theater. I will take ye e'ery night if that is your wish."

"Finlay…"

He held a hand up to stop the denial that was sure to spill from her lips. "What makes ye happy. No matter what 'tis, that is what I shall do."

She pursed her lips together and nodded, an odd look brightening her eyes. Finlay was unsure what to make of it, but he did not get the chance to dwell on that. As they exited the box to leave, a pair of women approached calling Willamina's name.

"Willamina!" A red-headed woman waved her gloved hand in the air to draw her attention. A brunette at her side matched her stride as they stopped in front of them. "We thought that was ye."

At his side, Willamina stiffened, her lips forming into a thin line.

"We wondered what had happened to ye. Ye disappeared in such haste. Who do we have here?" the brunette asked, eyeing him from head to toe.

He frowned. Though they clearly knew each other, it was obvious that Willamina was not happy to see them. He was getting ready to skirt them around the two women when she spoke up.

"Clarice, Viola, it has been some time since we've last seen each other."

"Indeed it has. Ye left in such a rush. Are ye no' going to introduce us to your companion."

Willamina sighed. "Clarice," she waved her hand in the direction of the woman with red hair. "Viola," she nodded to the other woman and then her gaze met his.

He gave her a small smile, assuring her that he was here for her. He gave her hand a squeeze of reassurance.

"This is Lord Primrose," Willamina continued.

The women's eyes rounded. "Lord Primrose?" Clarice said, and both women dipped into a curtsy.

"'Tis a pleasure to meet ye both. If ye will excuse us, we were just on our way home."

"Home?" Viola asked. "Ye are living here now, Willamina?"

"Have ye remarried? So soon?" Clarice chimed in.

Straightening her shoulders, Willamina addressed the women, her tone curt. "I havena, though Lord Primrose and I are engaged to be married. As ye both are well aware, my time of mourning has passed and I served it fully." She turned to him. "I shall like to go now."

"Of course, my dearest. Ladies, 'twas a pleasure."

"I would be wary of your finances around this one, my lord," Clarice said snidely.

He narrowed his eyes at the woman. "Pardon?"

She covered her mouth feigning shock. "Did she no' tell ye? I'm no' surprised," she whispered conspiratorially to Viola. "If I was run from my home and labeled a fraud, I wouldna tell anyone either."

He rounded up to the woman. "I would watch your tongue if I were ye. This isna Inverness, but I can have ye sent back there quickly enough," he whispered harshly, not wanting to draw any more attention to them than necessary.

He maneuvered Willamina around the two women, his hand firmly on the small of her back, which she kept ramrod straight until they were outside of the theater. She took a deep breath before hissing it out between her teeth.

"Hell's teeth. Pardon me for saying. What a couple of unpleasant harpies. Do I dare ask what that was about?"

"Och, those were two of my former friends from Inverness. One of them was one of my former husband's many lovers. The other abandoned me in my time of need."

He frowned. The two seemed full of vitriol. He knew there were things from her past that she had not spoken about. He also knew her cousin brought her to Edinburgh to find a husband. There had been no mention that she was forced to leave Inverness, or that she was a fraud.

Her arm rested in his as they waited for his carriage to pull up. He wanted to ask her about what they were referring to. To dig deeper into her past, but that was a conversation to be had outside the perimeter of prying ears.

Once inside the carriage, they sat side by side and he thought about the best way to broach the subject.

"I ken ye have questions. Rightly so," she said, wringing her hands in her lap.

He got the feeling that there was much more to the story than Clarice had mentioned. He considered himself a good judge of character. Willamina struck him as loyal and true. A fraud was the last thing that came to his mind when he thought of her character.

"Ye dinna have to tell me anything until ye are ready to do so."

She sighed in relief, a weight seemed to lift off her shoulders and she gave him a smile that brightened her eyes. "Ye are a good man, Finlay Primrose. I dinna believe I have e'er met another man like ye."

A stab of guilt pierced his gut. Just as much as she was holding back, so was he. He hadn't yet told her the real reason why he needed to marry. Aye, it was so he didn't have to deal with all the meddling mothers, but if it weren't for that damned clause in his father's will, he wouldn't have been at the garden party looking for a wife in the first place.

But the more time they spent together, the deeper he fell. And the clause slipped further and further from his mind. Because it wasn't the reason why he was getting married anymore.

Nay, it was the beautiful woman sitting next to him. The woman that consumed every hour, every minute, every second of his days.

He would tell her—when the time was right.

The urge to kiss her was strong. He wanted to capture her mouth in a kiss and never let her go.

"Ye flatter me, Mina."

She let out a yawn, her cheeks flushing.

"I fear I have tired ye out, my lady."

She chuckled. "Nay, no' at all, my lord," she teased, knowing he hated when she called him formally.

He supposed he deserved it, since he had just done the same to her.

"'Tis been a long day. The preparations have been time consuming. I am thankful for Clarissa's and Gwen's help. For certain I would no' have been able to plan e'erything without them."

"I am glad they have been of assistance. 'Tis no' long now. We just have to get through tomorrow."

"Fin?" She asked quietly, wringing her hands together.

"Aye?" He turned to her as best he could in the cramped space of the carriage.

"Are ye certain ye want to do this? I understand if ye dinna."

"Mina. I have ne'er been more certain of anything in my life."

"I hate lying to e'eryone. What will they say when they find out the truth."

"They willna."

"It canna last forever," she whispered.

"Why no'?" He took her hands in his, pulling her closer. "People have married for much less reason than what we are, and they have grown to love each other." He felt like he was grasping at limbs, trying to prevent himself from falling.

"Ye deserve to be happy."

He pulled her ever closer and he heard her hitch of breath.

"Ye make me happy."

"But I canna give ye what ye want."

Their faces were mere inches apart, he could feel her breath fan his face, and his cock jumped to life. "Kiss me."

He let the words hang in the air. It was not said as a demand, but a request. Minutes seemed to pass as she wrestled with whatever was going on in her mind. But he did not move away. Nor did he pull her closer.

Nay, if she wanted the kiss, she would be the one to accept it.

IN THE DARKNESS of the carriage, as they bobbled along the road, back to Buckwood Manor, Willamina held her breath. Had Finlay really just asked her to kiss him? And was her body aching to do just that?

Could she?

She did not have much experience with kissing. Gerard never kissed her other than their wedding night. She pushed all the thoughts of her late husband and all his unpleasantness out of her mind.

This was Finlay. He was not cruel like Gerard. He was kind and caring. And he wanted her.

Her.

Not anyone else.

Her.

Ignoring all the reasons floating around her mind as to why she should not, she leaned forward and tentatively touched her lips to his.

His fingers squeezed hers, but other than that, he made no move. She pushed her lips harder against his. She had the sudden urge to taste him. "Kiss me back," she whispered.

"Och, love. I thought ye would ne'er ask," he said against her mouth, before his hands left hers and cupped her face, slanting his mouth over hers, his tongue seeking entry as his fingers stroked the side of her face.

The feeling was purely erotic. Were kisses supposed to be so passionate? She opened her lips and his tongue swept inside.

She could not stop the moan that bubbled up from her throat as his mouth devoured hers. He left her panting for breath, her chest heaving.

The carriage came to a halt, and she could only assume they had arrived at Buckwood. She scooted back, taking a deep breath, trying to calm her nerves, her palm over her heart as her chest heaved. She swallowed hard. "I, I verra much enjoyed that," she whispered.

Finlay blew out a ragged breath and chuckled. "I am glad to hear that. I did as well." He loosened his cravat. "I suppose I should get ye inside, lest Gil wonders what we are doing."

She gasped. "We must no' have that."

He went to push the door open, and she stopped him by placing a hand on his arm. He looked at her, his brows raised in question.

"I have ne'er been kissed like that. Thank ye."

She felt like a fool for such an admission. And an even bigger fool for thanking him. He was going to think she was an imbecile.

Later that night as she lay in bed, her mind played over the kiss again and again. When she closed her eyes, visions of Finlay flooded her brain.

Sleep eluded her. Finlay consumed her. This was not how their plan was supposed to go. Feelings were not supposed to be involved.

But as the night wore on, the only thing she could think about was the next time Finlay could kiss her as passionately as he had in the carriage.

Och, this was not good. Not good at all. This muddied the waters. But no matter how she tried, she could not get Finlay out of her mind. His hands on her face, it was as if they had seared her skin. She could still feel his touch.

She turned on her side and punched the pillow in frustration. Not falling for Finlay Primrose was going to be much harder than she had originally anticipated.

How did one go from not wanting to get married, to suddenly thinking it may not be as bad an idea as she had once thought?

Ugh! There was no sleep to be had tonight so she shoved the covers away and wrapped herself in her robe. Sitting down on the plush window seat, she looked out into the moonlit night, wondering in what direction Rosewood Manor stood. It would not matter, it was not like she could see it anyway. But she would still like to know.

She drew her knees up and wrapped her arms around them and rested her chin, facing the window. Was Finlay suffering from her same predicament? She somehow doubted that. He seemed much more put together than she was.

As their wedding day drew near, she knew that she would have to confess the other reason why she had to leave Inverness. No thanks to Clarice and Viola. What were the chances of running into them at the theater?

Once again, she found herself shaking her head at how she ever believed they were her true friends. They were both cruel and self-serving. They only cared about themselves.

She vowed that she would tell Finlay the next day. With all the kindness he'd shown to her, it was only right that she told him the truth. She didn't want him to think that she had deceived him into marriage. Nay, he should have the option of calling the wedding off if he wanted.

She bit her lip. Finlay backing out of their union was not an option. She needed the wedding to happen. She had nothing. The ramifications of them not marrying would be dire for her.

She refused to be left to her cousin's devices. Being married off to someone where she had no choice in the matter was not something she wanted to deal with. Especially when that more than likely meant she also wouldn't have a say when it came to her assets.

Finlay was being more than kind and generous in letting her keep the management of her assets herself. It was something he didn't have to do, and it just made her fondness for him grow that much more.

Dawn could not come fast enough. She spent the wee hours of the morn moving from the window seat, to her vanity, to the chair by the fireplace, back to the window seat, her mind continuously playing out different scenarios of how Finlay would react when she told him the truth of her past. It was all frustrating. And when she finally spotted the first slivers of light, she breathed a sigh of relief. Soon, the household would wake up and she would have something to occupy her mind. They had dinner at Rosewood Manor this eve, and tonight would be the last night she spent at Buckwood Manor.

Joan had already started packing her things to be transferred to her new home. Trunks were lined up against the wall ready to be transported.

The thought of spending her days and nights in close proximity to Finlay had her pacing the floor once again.

This was very bad.

Very bad indeed.

CHAPTER TWELVE

"**B**ROTHER, YE HAVE returned." Finlay said dryly as Fingal whisked through the front door, Yvette entering right after.

His twin sneered. "And miss my dear brother's pre-wedding dinner party? How could I deny such a request?" Fingal pushed past him and made his way down the hall, Yvette following close on his heels. "Six o'clock, correct? I want to make sure we arena late," he called over his shoulder.

Even though Fingal no longer lived here, his bedroom was still set up for him. Unfortunately for Finlay, Fingal and Yvette took advantage of the space more often than he liked. Once Willamina moved in, he would put a stop to that. They had their own estate, there was no need for a room here any longer.

"Aye," Finlay mumbled. He pushed his hand through his hair as he watched his brother and his brother's wife disappear. His brother's countenance had him concerned. What was Fingal up to? He sighed. He had not the faintest idea, but he was sure there was something up his sleeve.

Mayhap he had come up with another ill-conceived speech. One made to tarnish his reputation in Willamina's eyes. It mattered naught. It was just a way for his brother to gain attention. Mayhap his wife could keep him under control, though Finlay highly doubted it. He could only wish that Fingal's antics did not ruin the whole night.

There were only a few hours left until everyone would gather and Willamina and Gil would arrive. One more night away from her and then she would be here. For good. Living at Rosewood Manor.

He could not stop thinking about their stolen kiss in the carriage the night before. He had left the choice up to her and whether or not she wanted to kiss him.

When she did, his body instantly reacted. It sprang to life as if it had been starving for her very kiss. He wanted to kiss her again. And again.

He hoped she felt the same way. Her reaction last night was sweet. If her late husband was still alive, he would hunt him down and beat the shite out of him for treating her so horribly. How could he deprive her from such pleasures?

Mayhap it was because he was not any good at it himself.

A knock sounded on his study door, and Gunn poked his head in. "Ye ready?"

He slapped the top of his desk, in his mind's eye thinking it was the late Lord Watson. "Aye. Is e'eryone else?"

"Ready as they e'er will be."

The five friends were heading to one of the clubs in the square for a couple of rounds of boxing. He was planning on working out some of his frustrations that stemmed from his brother.

At the club, they had claimed a ring in a room by themselves. The place smelled of sweat and leather.

"Can I just make it clear, gentlemen. No hitting me in the face today, aye?"

"Well, now ye are taking all the fun out of the fight, Primrose." Alexander laughed. "I, personally, would verra much like to punch ye in the face. Your smug look about your upcoming nuptials is tiring," he complained, but the corners of his mouth lifted in a smirk.

"If I recall correctly, 'twas no' that long ago, ye were in the same predicament," Finlay retorted.

"Aye," Nicholas chimed in. "And I really, really wanted to

punch ye in the face. Over and over again."

Alexander put his hands up in defeat. "Hey now, your sister loves me. She wouldna have let ye do any such damage."

Nicholas snorted. "She canna stop what she is not around for."

Back and forth, they took shots at each other as they taped up their hands.

"I saw Fingal moping around earlier. He and his wife will be in attendance this eve?" Malcolm asked.

"Aye," Finlay said with a sigh, and finished wrapping the tape around his wrist. He cut the piece off with his teeth and smacked his hands together. "Who is first?"

Alexander hopped up and gave him a light punch in the shoulder. "Come on, pretty lad. I promise I willna mar that beautiful face of yours." His head snapped to Nicholas as the words came out of his mouth and he looked like he wanted to take them back. "No offense brother."

"None taken. But I am glad that I dinna have to worry about hitting ye in the face when my turn comes."

"Great," Alexander mumbled as he climbed through the ropes behind Finlay.

Fists up, they circled each other. Finlay threw out a jab, and then blocked the incoming punch with his shoulder. He returned with a left hook to Alexander's gut.

"Ooof!" He shoved Finlay away and they rounded up again. "Ye ken, I liked it better when I could hit ye in the face."

Laughter erupted in the room as they continued sparring. When they switched out, Finlay still had frustrations he wanted to rid himself of. In the corner, hanging from the ceiling was a punching bag filled with sand. He approached it and pounded the hell out of it. By the time he was done, he was breathing heavily, his knuckles bruised, and his brow sweaty.

His friends looked at him like he had lost his mind. Except Gunn. He looked at him with pride. Not surprising since Gunn was the fighter in the group.

"Feel better?" he asked.

Finlay gave him a curt nod and collapsed in a chair and watched as Alexander and Nicholas went at it in the ring.

"Anything I can help with?" Gunn asked.

"Nay, thank ye though. Just family stuff. That hopefully will be resolved once Willamina and I are wed."

Gunn frowned but did not say anything further.

"Ow!" Alexander snarled as Nicholas connected with a right hook to the jaw. "If my face is all black and blue tomorrow, ye are going to have to answer to your sister."

Nicholas laughed. "Are ye saying ye need your wife to stand up for ye?" He swung again, but Alexander ducked out of the way and countered with his own hook, but Nicholas stepped back and the swing went wide, connecting with nothing.

"I liked ye better when ye werena my brother-in-law."

Peals of laughter filled the air, and Finlay found himself finally relaxing. This was what he needed. An afternoon out with his friends to take his mind off of everything that was happening.

"All right, ye two. Both of your wives will have our heads if ye both return with your faces smashed in," Malcolm called out.

Nicholas jumped out of the ring, swiping the back of his hand against his bloodied lip. Alexander followed, his right eye already starting to swell.

"One final toast before we head back," Gunn announced, pouring a dram of whisky for everyone. "Finlay, may your days be forever happy, and your nights e'en happier. Slainte!"

A chorus of cheers rose up and they all drank.

Finlay was thankful for the day. And the toast. If only his friends knew the truth. They would be trying to talk him out of committing to such a farce.

But no matter what, he would not back out.

And it was not because he needed to marry. That clause had become secondary to what he really wanted.

Nay, everything revolved around Willamina. He would not let her down.

WILLAMINA, FINLAY, ALL his friends, their wives, his brother and his wife, along with Gil were all seated at the table in the dining hall. They had just finished dessert which consisted of the most divine pistachio ice that Willamina had ever tasted.

Just as the women were getting ready to step away with a cordial, and the men with their brandy, Fingal stood up, his spoon clinking against the crystal glass he was holding.

"Before we all retire, I thought I would say a word to the *lucky* couple."

He put an odd emphasis on the word lucky and Willamina sought Finlay's eyes. They were focused on his brother, his brows creased.

"As ye ken," Fingal continued, pushing his chair back and standing. "My dear twin brother is to be married tomorrow."

A cheer rose from the attendees, and he smiled. Not a particularly pleasant smile, Willamina noted.

"And while Lady Watson is lovely, indeed. more than capable of catching the eye of any man in the city, has no' anyone wondered why, Finlay, who has notoriously said he willna marry, has had a sudden change of heart?"

"Brother," Finlay growled.

"Och, *brother*," Fingal countered.

Yvette placed a hand on her husband's arm, but he shook it off.

It was like watching a tennis match. Willamina's eyes shifted from one brother to the next. Their identical appearances only differentiated by the complete opposite looks on each of their faces.

"I only think it proper that Lady Watson knows what brought about the change."

"Fingal," Finlay stood abruptly. "That is enough."

Willamina had never seen Finlay's face so red. He was getting most upset. Whatever could Fingal say that could anger him so?

"'Tis no' enough, dear brother. The truth should be brought to light. Lady Watson," Fingal turned and addressed her. "What my brother has failed to tell ye, and is obviously no' wanting me to tell ye either," he smirked at Finlay, an evil, snide smile that made him look positively nasty. "My brother *needs* to marry ye. Our father has dictated it so."

"Fingal, for all that is holy, that is enough!" Finlay shouted.

Willamina was confused. Early on Finlay had said, well, no, he just said he wanted to be off the market so as to get away from all the meddling mothers. She thought back to their earlier conversations. She had believed there was something he was holding back, but she was keeping her own secret, so she couldn't fault him.

"Without ye, he loses his title."

Willamina sucked in a breath, and a silence filled the room.

Until Finlay launched himself across the table and pinned his brother to the floor. "Ye fucking arsehole." He landed three solid punches to Fingal's face before Gunn and Malcolm pulled him off and held him away.

Fingal just laughed as blood streamed from his nose and Yvette dropped to her knees beside him.

Willamina did not know what to do. Fingal's words played over in her mind.

Even though they both knew their union was a ruse, she thought they had been honest with each other as to the reasons.

Even as she thought that, she knew it wasn't true. They both were hiding things. But using her to keep his title? How was that even possible? How does one lose their title? That seemed like something he should have told her about.

She pinched the bridge of her nose, a headache suddenly making her head spin. She looked around. Finlay was cursing up a storm at his brother, while Fingal just laughed. His friends were trying to calm him down, and Clarissa and Gwen stared in horror.

Willamina backed away from the table. And for once, Gil

offered support when he stepped up and guided her to the door.

"Willamina!" Finlay called out. "Let me explain."

She squared her shoulders. "I should verra much like to leave now. I have much to consider."

"Ye canna consider without all of the facts. Please," he begged. The pain on his face tugged at her heart.

There was more to the story than the clipped version Fingal spoke of. But she did not want to hear it tonight.

"Tomorrow morning. Come to Buckwood Manor. Tonight, I would just like to think. Good eve."

And with that, Gil pushed her out the door and into their waiting carriage.

"Cousin—"

Willamina stopped him with a hand up in the air. "Dinna. I dinna want to talk about it tonight." She angrily swiped at the tears that began to fall.

She found it ironic that she had vowed to tell Finlay the truth about her past tonight and she hoped in doing so, that she wouldn't lose him. But in a twist of fate, she found out his truth, and now she was the one running away.

If the marriage was to be on paper only, why did it matter the reason?

And why did the real reason hurt so much?

CHAPTER THIRTEEN

FINLAY GLARED AT Fingal. "Get out," he shouted. "Get the fuck out!"

His brother stood, sneering as he spat blood onto the floor. "Gladly. My work here is done."

Finlay lunged again, but Gunn was ready and stopped his advance, shoving him into a chair while Malcolm escorted Fingal and Yvette out of the room, then shut the door behind him.

"Well," Alexander said. "I am guessing that did no' go as planned."

Gwen and Clarissa stood. "We shall take our leaves as well. We will see ye in the morn."

The men watched and waited as the women escaped to the salon or wherever they were going to go to get away from them.

With just the five of them remaining, they all took a seat. The table was a mess. Glasses had been spilled and plates scattered. Finlay noticed a couple of pieces of dinnerware had been shattered.

He cocked his head to the side, running his tongue over his teeth and he tried to slow down his simmering anger. "Gentlemen, I do apologize for my behavior." He blew out a breath and shook his head. "This night took quite the turn, I will admit."

"What was your brother referring to?" Malcolm asked.

"I should have been the one to tell Willamina. In my own way," Finlay spat, disgusted as much with himself as he was at his brother.

"Color me confused," Alexander remarked, as he grabbed a bottle of wine from the side table and righted the glasses to fill them.

"Ye all remember my father. He always had a wit about him. This time he, by way of his will, demanded that I marry before I turn twenty-eight, or I forfeit the title to Fingal."

"What?" Gunn asked. "Can he do that?"

"'Tis his will, he can do whatever he deemed fit." He drank his glass of wine in one long swallow, and Alexander leaned over to refill it.

"So, ye dinna love Willamina—Lady Watson?" Nicholas asked.

"That is the thing. I do. Well, I dinna know if 'tis yet love, but I," he paused, looking for the right words to say. "I have feelings for Willamina that run true."

"There ye go," Alexander said. "Ye just need to explain it to her so she understands. Women are fickle creatures, but their minds get all befuddled when it comes to matters of the heart. She will accept your explanation, no harm, no foul."

"I do take offense to ye describing women as such, Alexander. That is my sister ye speak of."

Alexander's look of annoyance drew a smile from Nicholas.

"I fear 'twill no' be so easy as to explain my actions. 'Tis complicated."

"Why no'?"

It was bad enough that he had to tell his friends about his deception. He was not about to divulge Willamina's reasoning for accepting their agreement.

He had to talk to her. Before he said anything else to anyone, they needed to talk. Tomorrow was their wedding day.

And come hell or high water, he planned to be married.

"I care no' to speak of this any further this eve. As instructed, I will visit with Willamina in the morn and hopefully we will clear up any confusion." He stalked to the door. "If ye will excuse me. I apologize for the ruined e'ening."

Not waiting for any acknowledgment from his friends, he swept out of the room, stopping by his study to snag a bottle of whisky and a glass, then retreated to his room. He dropped into the chair in front of the fireplace and poured himself a healthy serving of whisky.

He cursed Fingal. He should have known that his good-for-naught brother was up to something. The bastard would not let it be until either Fingal got the title or Finlay married.

"Shite!" He threw the glass into the fireplace and watched the flames spark as crystal shattered everywhere.

This whole thing was a mess. Tomorrow, he would be at Willamina's doorstep, begging if he had to.

Gil would surely take immense pleasure in watching him grovel.

But grovel he would if that is what it took to get Willamina to see the truth.

AFTER A SLEEPLESS night, Finlay knocked on the door of Buckwood Manor just after nine o'clock. It was early, but not so early as Willamina would not be up and already broken her fast. He could not wait any longer to call. The night had already seemed to last an eternity.

"Lord Primrose," Domenic greeted as he opened the door. "Lady Watson is expecting ye."

Finlay tried to hide his smile. That she was waiting for him could only mean good things, he had to assume. The opposite was not something he wanted to entertain, and he pushed any negative thoughts out of his head.

Domenic led him to the parlor, where Willamina sat with a teacup perched in her hand.

"My lady, Lord Primrose has arrived."

Her hand shook ever so slightly at the announcement, causing the tea to slosh in the cup before she stabilized it.

"Thank ye, Domenic. Ye may go."

Finlay watched as the butler disappeared down the hall.

"Well, are ye going to sit or shall we speak with ye standing at the door?"

Finlay jumped into action, mumbling an apology as he sat down at the seat across from her.

"Tea?" she asked.

He declined and waited for her to speak. He wanted to start the conversation but felt that it was important for her to take control, so he let her have it.

"I understand that our," her tongue darted out and wet her lips, "dinner last eve didna go as anticipated."

He chortled. There was no other reaction that would be suitable. "'Tis an understatement, indeed."

"My night was spent sleepless and in deep reflection. Playing our deal over and over in my head." She sipped her tea, her eyes focused on the window.

"And what have ye come to conclude?" he asked, a hint of anxiousness tinging his voice.

"Our arrangement, as ye will, was one agreed upon out of need, not out of want. My cousin insisted I marry, and I only wanted to keep what was rightfully mine. But ye, ye on the other hand, said that ye needed to get married to take ye off the marriage mart."

"Aye."

"But that wasna exactly true, was it?" Sad blue eyes clashed with his.

He took a deep breath as he picked at imaginary lint on his trousers as he thought of the best way to answer her question. In the end, he could only give her the truth.

"Whilst 'tis true that I wanted to be out of sight of all the young women looking to make a good, suitable match, I also had another reason, which I stupidly withheld from ye. Willamina, I dinna know what I was thinking. I was being daft, really."

"Ye played me for a fool."

"Nay. Absolutely no'."

She set the saucer down with a clatter and stood up. Pacing in front of the window. "I dinna ken why I e'en care. We were ne'er a love match. It was strictly business. Your reason for the union didna really matter any more than mine did. In the end we both would get what we wanted." She spun and pierced him with an intense stare. "I just wish ye had been honest with me. Be honest with me now. Was what your brother spoke the truth?"

He nodded in defeat. "Aye. 'Twas. When our father passed, neither of us knew what was in his will. He had kept it a secret and neither of us paid any heed. Until the reading that is. It stated that if I dinna wed by my twenty-eighth birthday, I would forfeit the title of earl and it would move to Fingal."

"Why would your father demand such a thing?"

He shrugged, shaking his head from side to side. "I dinna ken. It made no sense really. And honestly, I had not paid it any heed, until the nearing of my birthday. I spoke with his solicitor and the will was iron-clad. There was no way around it."

"So ye decided to find a fool?"

"Nay," he stood and approached her, grasping her hands in his, thankful that she did not pull away. "The garden party when we first met? That was the first party I had gone to. I abhor attending such affairs. But I went in the hopes of finding someone that I would find interesting. Someone that I could possibly see spending my future with."

She sniffled, her shoulders rising and falling before shifting her gaze to the window once again.

"Willamina."

Her eyes returned to his.

"E'eryone that I had met that day didna hold my interest. They were either too meek and timid, or too boring, or too passive. Until I met ye. And in my mind, I saw our future."

"And an end to your potential problem."

"Aye, that too, but it was ye. Ye and your personality. Your independence that drew me to ye."

She ducked her head, but not before he saw her wavering smile.

"When I saw that your cousin was forcing ye to wed, and ye stated ye had no such want, I thought we could solve each other's problems, and mayhap enjoy each other's company in the process."

"Ye didna e'en ken me or naught about me."

He chuckled. "Ye showed me more fire in that short interaction we had in the maze than the lot of lasses that had been pushed on me all day put together." He squeezed her hands, and his heart jumped when her fingers squeezed back.

"At first, aye, 'twas a business deal. Made in both of our favors. But the longer we spent together, it became less about business and more about ye."

"I told ye I dinna need a husband." She whispered.

"I know."

"Will your title be enough? I canna give ye the relationship ye desire. The one ye deserve." Her eyes bore into his as if she were trying to make him see.

"My title be damned. Would I like to keep it? Aye. But ye ken what I want to keep more?"

She slowly shook her head, her lower lip quivering slightly.

"Ye. I want to keep ye more."

She closed her eyes and he brought his hand up to sweep her hair behind her ear. "I canna stop thinking about the kiss we shared. I ken ye felt it, too."

She turned into his hand, placing a kiss on his palm. "I have my own sullied past," she whispered.

"I dinna care." He wrapped an arm around her waist and pulled her to him.

"'Tis ugly. Ye got a glimpse at the theater. But believe me when I say that I am no' nor have I e'er been a fraud."

"It doesna matter. Whate'er it is, we shall work through it. And I promise no' to keep any more secrets from ye, Mina. Just tell me ye will marry me still."

MINA. HE HAD called her by the nickname he'd given her earlier and it went straight to her heart. As they stood there, near the window, so close their fronts rested against each other, her breath coming in short gasps, she looked into his ice-blue eyes.

He had told her the truth, but had not demanded she do the same. She had not been untruthful about anything that she had told him, but she had left many aspects out.

However, this could be her salvation. Did it really matter that he was doing it to keep his title?

Nay. Not when she had agreed to the union to keep her own assets.

They were practically doing the same thing.

"Aye," she whispered, her mind made up.

"Aye, as in ye will marry me?" he asked, sounding incredulous.

She nodded and he pulled her even closer though she thought that was impossible. And as his head dropped to hers, he captured her mouth in a searing kiss that matched the one the other night. Something deep in her belly stirred.

As if awakening. And this time when his tongue sought entry, she did not resist. She gave herself into his kiss, pushing her hands through his hair and his hands moved down her back, slid lower, cupping her buttocks and pulling her closer to him.

A throat cleared in the doorway, and Willamina practically tumbled backward trying to put distance between her and Finlay. "Cousin!" she exclaimed, hand on her heaving chest.

"Shall I assume by that display I just witnessed that the wedding is still taking place?" He glared at Finlay. "And I will say that if ye say nay, after what just happened, my cousin is now compromised, and ye will marry her."

"Gil, dinna be obtuse. And dinna threaten Finlay." She looked back at Finlay and was taken aback by the emotion on his face. Mayhap they could have a happy marriage after all. If his kisses were a preview of what was to come, she could only imagine. She shook her head to clear it from her straying thoughts. "The wedding will go on as scheduled."

Finlay pulled her back to him and kissed her neck, causing her to shiver and her skin to heat.

Gil scoffed. "Ye are no' married yet, Primrose. Save it until after your vows. I willna have ye defiling my cousin in my home."

Willamina could not help but roll her eyes as her cousin spun and left the room. Noticing the time, she gasped. "We must make haste. The time for our ceremony draws near and neither of us is ready. I am to meet with Gwen and Clarissa to help me get ready soon."

Finlay gave her a charming smile. "Fear no'. I can bring ye to them. Gather whate'er ye need. I will load it onto the carriage."

"Thank ye. I shall fetch Joan as well."

She rushed out of the room, fearing her face was red as the skin of a ripened apple.

In her room, she rang the bell to call for Joan. Her body was a bundle of nerves. She tried to sit and wait for her maid to arrive, but she could not sit still. Finlay had set her nerves afire and she was not sure what to do about it.

Guilt still niggled its way under her skin for not revealing her past to him. There was also the part of her that felt like a hypocrite. And for all her thoughtful bravado earlier, in the back of her mind, she still worried that if she told him the truth of what had happened before, that he would call the ceremony off. That couldn't happen. No matter what, she needed to get married. Today.

"My lady?" Joan appeared in the doorway. "Are ye unwell?"

"Nay, nay, I am fine. We must make haste. We will be traveling with Fin—Lord Primrose for the ceremony."

A huge smile broke out on Joan's face. "So 'tis still happening?" She nearly squealed with excitement, clapping her hands together.

"Hush, Joan! He may hear ye."

"Sorry, my lady," she whispered. "This is good, aye?"

Willamina blew out a breath but could not keep the happy smile off her face. It was good, was it not? "I believe so, Joan. Now let us gather e'erything we need for the day. Lord Primrose will send for the rest of our things later."

Quickly, they chose the items needed, including the boxes from the modiste that contained her wedding dress and the lacy nightdresses the woman had designed, even though she would not be wearing them.

Or maybe she would.

An hour later, her trunk and boxes had been loaded onto the back of Finlay's carriage and the three of them were tucked inside on their way to Rosewood Manor.

Gwen and Clarissa met them at the door and whisked Willamina away into the room Clarissa and Alexander were staying in whilst they visited. In a whirlwind, she was transformed into a beautiful bride.

As she looked at her reflection in the mirror, she couldn't help but smile; tears threatened to spill. She had never felt or looked so beautiful. This was such a contrast from her first marriage.

"Dinna cry, Willamina. What is wrong?" Clarissa asked. "Do ye no' like it? We can change whate'er ye are unhappy with."

Willamina shook her head. "Nay. 'Tis the opposite. I love it. Thank ye."

Gwen settled in beside her and patted her knee. "Tears of joy are the best thing. I am glad that ye and Finlay resolved the incident from last night. I am sure Fingal had his reasons for airing such grievances during dinner, but 'twas no' the right time to do so."

Willamina nodded. She could only surmise that his ultimate

goal was to stop the wedding. If he prevented that from moving forward and Finlay didn't marry in time, then the title would go to Fingal. A purely selfish move. But titles and money made one act addlebrained sometimes.

A knock sounded, and Alexander's voice called out from the other side. "Ready? I am to bring ye to the chapel."

Willamina took a deep breath and blew it out slowly. For a wedding that was only for paper, she felt just as nervous as if it were real. All those around them thought it was real and she supposed some of that weighed on her shoulders as well. Even after Fingal's outburst, Finlay's friends didn't think any differently. Mayhap he had taken them aside and explained things to them and they were acting how he wanted them to.

She could not stop the little voice in her head whispering to her that she wished it could be real. Of all the men she had met, Finlay was by far leagues ahead. A greater match she couldn't wish for. And Gil was happy that he would finally be rid of his cousin and any responsibilities that came with her.

Her heart seemed to rule her lately. It was slowly letting Finlay chip away at the walls she had built around it. And she wasn't even upset about it. Instead she found herself looking forward to the future. Something she hadn't done in a very long time.

Clarissa clasped her hands and pulled her up. "Ye look beautiful. Finlay will be speechless."

And he was. When she rounded the corner on Gil's arm and began walking down the aisle at the small chapel tucked away into a corner on the estate, Finlay's mouth dropped open before he snapped it shut his Adam's apple bobbing, the tip of his tongue darting out to wet his lips. Those ice-blue eyes locked on hers and for the first time, she believed this was real.

CHAPTER FOURTEEN

INLAY NEVER BELIEVED angels walked this earth—until
Willamina Watson appeared in the aisle walking toward him
on this, their wedding day.

She was a vision of beauty in her cream-colored gown, fitting
as it wasn't her first marriage. The lace bodice and silk skirt fit her
perfectly. He looked forward to peeling the gloves off her slender
arms, the urge to kiss the pulse point on each wrist strong.

His tongue felt heavy in his mouth, and as she stepped closer
and closer, he lost the ability to form words.

When Gil stepped forward and handed Willamina over to
Finlay, his breath caught in his throat as he caught her hand in
his.

She smiled shyly as she looked at him through her lashes.

And his heart burst into a thousand pieces.

He had been a fool if he thought that he would ever get out
of this arrangement with his heart intact.

Later, as he held her in his arms and they danced in celebration, he whispered against her ear, "Have I told ye how beautiful
ye look today?"

Her musical laughter floated on the air. "Only e'ery few
minutes, my lord."

He growled low. "And I shall tell ye the same going forward."

Rosewood Manor was decorated for the grandest of balls. His
staff had taken a lot of care to ensure the house was filled with
beautiful flowers and arrangements. On the morrow, they would

surely be the talk of the city.

Anyone of importance was in attendance for the party and now that the night had worn on, the crowd was starting to dwindle.

Finlay could sense Willamina's trepidation. As they bid their guests a good night, she began to get fidgety, a trait he had noticed she did when her nerves began to surface.

"Ye have no need to be nervous, Mina. The night is yours." It killed him to say that. But he had made a promise to her. He would not force her into anything she did not want. Now that they were married, his mindset hadn't changed. He would stay true to his word.

She would need to make the first steps to change their rela-tionship—no matter how hard it would be to sit and wait, hoping that it would happen.

"Soon we shall leave for Primrose Castle."

"Are we no' staying here, at Rosewood?"

"Nay. With all of our guests staying here, no one expects us to spend our wedding night here. At Primrose we will have privacy."

"I see. Will Joan go with us?" she asked, her voice a slightly higher pitch than usual.

"No' tonight. But she will arrive in the next few days to assist ye with whate'er ye may need."

She rolled her lips inward.

"What are ye thinking?" he asked, sipping his glass of cham-pagne.

"Naught really."

"Mina. I may no' ken e'erything about ye, but I can tell when something is bothering ye." He grabbed her hand. "And some-thing is definitely bothering ye."

"Tis no' anything I wish to speak about at this time."

"My lord and lady, your carriage awaits to take ye to Prim-rose Castle."

"Thank ye, Archibald." He stood and held out his hand to

Willamina. "My lady."

Her eyes were bright as she accepted his hand and allowed him to pull her up. And, getting lost in the moment, he planted a kiss on her lips, before quickly pulling away.

She brought her fingers up to her mouth, which was lifted in a smile. Mayhap there was hope for them yet.

WILLAMINA HAD SO many thoughts running through her head on the carriage ride over to Primrose Castle. Finlay sat beside her, his thigh touching hers, heating her whole body. Every time the carriage jostled, he bumped into her, making the space between them less.

"I look forward to seeing Primrose Castle," she said, trying to change the subject so she would stop thinking about his closeness.

He gave her a smile. "I look forward to showing it to ye. 'Twill be yours to run as ye see fit from this point on, but ye will have a few days before having to take on such a task."

She did not plan on taking over the Primrose Castle household, or any of Finlay's holdings' households. Those were his properties and should remain that way. The only household she was worried about was Warton House back in Inverness.

Any other residence belonged to Finlay and she did not expect him to turn anything over to her. Those should go to his wife.

Though she was his wife, his holdings should go to his *real* wife. The one that he would have in the future.

But *I* am his real wife. They had the papers to prove it.

"Ye needn't do that, Finlay. I shouldna be made responsible for Primrose Castle. 'Tis your holding. It belongs in your family."

His hand clasped hers. "And in my family it remains."

"Finlay."

"Willamina."

She noticed he called her by her full name instead of the nickname he had taken to calling her lately.

"This is no' real, remember."

His ice-blue eyes clouded. "I remember," he said stiffly. "However, for it to be believable for those around us, we still need to follow the steps that all newly married couples follow."

She nodded.

The carriage came to a halt, jolting them into each other again. She straightened, trying to put a little distance between them.

The door swung open and Finlay exited, turning with a hand out to her to assist. Placing her hand in his, his fingers wrapped around hers as she stepped out of the carriage.

Her breath caught at the sight in front of her. Primrose Castle was a large tower house. Torches lit the exterior and also along the pathway leading up to the entry. She could hear the rush of water, letting her know they were close to the coast. It was too dark to see, so she would have to wait until the morrow to see more.

She followed him through the huge arched doorway, which opened to a massive space. Large arched windows blanketed the door. The floors were wood, polished to a shiny hue. She craned her neck to look at the tall ceilings. The walls were papered in a pretty multi-color flowered pattern with a yellow background.

"My lord," a new butler that Willamina didn't recognize addressed Finlay. "I have taken the initiative to move the lady's belongings into the master suite."

"Thank ye, Richard. And may I present to ye my wife, Willamina, Lady Primrose."

It felt so odd to be presented as a wife. Also, to no longer be called Lady Watson. The last hold her late husband held on her was now gone. She would never have to be referred to as that name again. A sense of relief washed over her at that realization.

She dipped her head in greeting. "'Tis a pleasure to meet ye,

Richard."

He bowed, and disappeared through one of the doors.

"Shall we?" Finlay waved a hand toward the stairs.

In this house, a center staircase, so wide it appeared that eight people could climb it side by side, was the focal point of the entryway. The stairs were a rich, dark wood, with plush red carpet covering the center.

She inhaled a deep breath, and nodded. Up the stairs, they took a right and walked all the way to the end of the wood-paneled hall. Pausing in front of a set of massive double doors, Finlay gave her a wink before pushing the doors open and stepping aside to allow her entry.

Inside the room, her eyes widened. One massive four-poster bed was centered against the far wall. Plush pillows were piled high on top of a dark blue coverlet.

She looked around the room, searching for another bed, but found none.

"Finlay…"

"Och, aye. I know what ye are going to say. Though we are no' at Rosewood, we still need to pass as wed in e'ery way. We canna do that in separate rooms. I shall sleep on the floor, and none will be the wiser."

She was mortified at his statement. "Ye will do no such thing." She eyed the bed. Its sheer size would fit four people. They were but two. She would probably regret the words that were about to spill from her lips, but there was no way that she was going to have the earl sleep on the floor. In his own home no less. Straightening her shoulders, she met his gaze. "The bed appears to be more than large enough to accommodate the both of us. I see no harm in sharing it."

She did see the harm, but she was not about to admit that to Finlay.

He had a pained look on his face. Mayhap he did not like her suggestion.

"I, er, I am no' sure that is the best idea."

"Ye canna possibly sleep on the floor. I willna have it."

"Mina, I dinna think ye ken the full breadth of what ye are suggesting."

Finlay seemed visibly upset. Well, mayhap upset wasn't the correct word. Perturbed? Nay. Distressed. Aye. That seemed a better fit for whatever emotions were dancing across his handsome face as he loosened his cravat and yanked it off his neck.

"I do, and I insist," she pushed.

His eyes settled on the table that was loaded with dried meats, cheeses, and a decanter of wine. "It seems to have gotten quite warm in here." He moved to the table and poured the wine. "Would ye like a glass?"

Thinking the wine may help settle her overactive nerves, she nodded. She accepted the glass with shaky hands. Now that they were wed, she did want to clarify some things. Taking a long sip of wine, she thought about the best way to approach the subject. Finally deciding that frankness was what was needed, she pushed forward.

"Finlay? Might I ask ye something?"

He sat in the mahogany armchair and crossed his legs. "Of course."

She took a deep breath and blew it out through her teeth, trying to gain the courage to voice what was weighing on her mind. "'Tis more than likely no' my place to ask, but I canna seem to move forward without putting forth the question." She paced the length of the room, her feet unwilling to stand in the same spot. "Will ye be bringing mistresses home?"

Wine burst from Finlay's mouth as he sputtered, his eyes wide. "Pardon? Certainly I misheard your question."

She turned to him and met his eyes. "Your mistresses. Will ye be bringing them here?"

His eyes grew dark and his mouth set into a thin line as he searched her face. "Willamina," he pushed off the chair and approached her.

She took a step back and he stopped his advance.

"I have no plans to take a mistress. A lover. A dalliance. Whate'er ye would like to call it. I will no' break my vows."

She shook her head. "Ye dinna have to deny yourself. I only ask that ye dinna parade them in front of me."

He fisted his hands on his hips. "Where are these questions coming from?"

Worrying her lower lip, she looked away. She didn't want him to see the pain that was surely evident in her eyes.

"Mina." He closed the distance between them.

When she stepped back, he met her step.

"Tell me," he demanded quietly.

FINLAY HELD HIS patience in check as he waited for Willamina to answer him. She backed away another step, and he followed. She would not escape him nor this conversation. A conversation that she had begun. Need he remind her of that?

With her back against the wall, she couldn't retreat any further and he waited. So close. He was so close to her, but he didn't touch her. Tempting as it was. He wanted to reach out, stroke her cheek. Wrap her in an embrace while he whispered that everything would be well.

But he couldn't. Not when she had something weighing on her mind so heavily.

"Is this about your first marriage?"

Tears made her eyes glisten and she blinked rapidly to try to disperse them. She pressed her lips together, looking everywhere in the room except at him, before finally throwing her hands up in the air. "I believe I mentioned afore, my late husband was no' a good man to me."

He nodded in encouragement.

She wet her lips before continuing. "Our marriage was no'

one of love, which isna necessarily uncommon. Sometimes love will develop, but for us, it didna. Nay, for him it didna, however, I grew to love Gerard. The feelings were one-sided and that ne'er changed. He found himself more interested in other," she paused as if it pained her to continue, "In other more experienced women. More beautiful women. He had no qualms about traipsing them in front of me. Being as loud and rambunctious as they could whilst closed away in his bedchamber," she sniffled.

"Willamina—"

She held her hand up and shook her head, swiping at her tears angrily. "I canna do that again. I ken our marriage is a ruse. But, I am sorry. I willna allow that again."

The look of pure betrayal and pain on her face was more than he could bear. He wrapped her in his arms as she sobbed into his chest, her breaths shallow and ragged. He said naught. Just stroked her hair in comfort as he waited for her to calm down.

When the sobs subsided and all that was left was sniffling, he rested his chin on her head. "I vow to ye, Mina, I wouldna show ye such disrespect. Your late husband was a vile man of low character to do such a disgrace to ye."

He handed her his handkerchief and she dabbed at her eyes and then her nose, which was now a bit pink from her crying. "That means a lot to me. I understand it is a sacrifice for ye to agree to such a demand."

His hands on her shoulders, he forced her to look at him. "'Tis no sacrifice, Mina. I mean it."

Her eyes bore into his, as if the deeper she tried to dig the more information she would find.

"I am an honest man." He dipped his head sheepishly. "With the exception of my father's will and I promise I will ne'er hide anything from ye again. Ken what I am saying as the truth. What we are doing is no' a sacrifice. Taking a mistress has ne'er and will ne'er cross my mind. That is no' something I would lie about."

She nodded and took a step to the side, out of his arms and he felt the loss of contact immediately. Dropping his hands, he watched her. He could see she needed her space, and he would grant her that.

"I think I would like some more wine," she said quietly.

He grabbed the decanter off the table and fetched her glass from the mantel and filled it before handing it over to her.

"My offer to sleep on the floor still stands."

She took a long sip of wine and then shook her head. "The bed will be fine." She bit her lower lip and he could almost see the wheels of her mind working. "Though I have an idea, if I may?"

He lifted his hand and shrugged. "Of course."

Walking to the bed, she drew down the covers all the way to the foot of the bed. "How many pillows do ye sleep with?"

What was she getting at? "One," he answered.

She turned back to the bed and gathered the pillows, leaving one on each side of the bed. Climbing on the mattress, she arranged the pillows in a line in the center, creating a barrier between them, while he admired her round bottom. He didn't feel guilty about it one bit.

He dipped his head, hiding his smile. He had meant what he said when he told her he would never take advantage of her. But if a physical 'wall' between them set her mind to ease, then he would allow it. Whatever made her comfortable he was fine with.

If his friends could see him now they would never let him live it down. Before Alexander had married Clarissa, he was the one in their group that had a continuous stream of lassies warming his bed. But Finlay was a close second. But once he'd met Willamina he'd been like a whipped puppy when it came to her. Truly, the thought of taking a mistress disgusted him. Why would he do such a thing when he had perfection sitting right before him?

She looked over at him warily. "I hope ye dinna mind?"

Giving her what he hoped was a smile that would put her at ease, he shook his head. "No' at all. Are ye hungry or are ye ready to retire for the night?"

"I think I have had enough excitement for the day and would

like to go to bed."

"I shall take me leave so that ye may ready yourself for bed in private." He turned to leave, but she called him back.

"Finlay?"

He stopped and turned to her. "Aye?"

Wringing her hands together, her cheeks flushed. "I, um, er." She blew out an exasperated breath. "I canna undo my gown."

"Ah, that makes sense. Shall I call someone for assistance? I know Joan isna here yet, but I am certain another maid can help ye with what ye need."

She shook her head. "That willna do. Just like we need to share the room, how do ye think it would look if ye send someone up to help me undress? On our wedding night?"

He chuckled. "I suppose ye are right. What shall we do then?"

She turned, giving him her back, and swept her hair to the front. "If ye could undo the buttons, I can take care of the rest."

For a moment, he was frozen in his spot. "Right." He approached her and with shaky fingers began releasing the buttons. With each button, more of her back was exposed to him. He wanted to run his tongue down her spine. His body roared to life. Her smell was divine and he inhaled deeply, like he wanted to have her assaulting all his senses. Pale, soft skin was uncovered in front of his eyes and he had to bite back a moan. The urge to pull her against him, to nuzzle her neck. To spin her around and bare her breasts to him was strong.

But he was a man of his word. As he undid the last of the buttons, which were very near to her buttocks, it took all of his strength not to squeeze the globes of her arse in his hands. He stepped back. "That should suffice. Whilst ye finish, I will just face the wall over here." He pointed to the other side of the room. "Ye can let me know when ye are set."

Stiffly, he walked over to the fireplace and stared into the flames.

Flames that matched his desire.

CHAPTER FIFTEEN

WILLAMINA HAD HELD her breath as Finlay's fingers brushed along her skin, working their way down her back as he slowly unfastened the buttons of her dress. He caused goose pimples to rise on her skin and she hoped he didn't notice her reaction.

She looked over her shoulder. True to his word, Finlay stood near the fireplace, staring into the flames, his back to her.

Flashbacks of her first wedding night flitted through her mind. There was no romance. No consideration for her feelings. Gerard had ordered her to strip and then pushed her roughly onto the bed, taking what had then belonged to him, not caring the pain it caused her. When he was done, he left the room and she didn't see him until the next morning.

Finlay would be a caring lover. She believed that with all her heart and being. He was too kind. And the way he looked at her with desire pooling in his eyes set her stomach aflutter. He tried to hide his feelings, but she got glimpses of them before he quickly schooled his looks.

Laying with Finlay would most certainly be a different experience. A divine experience. One that, once she had a taste, she would forever long for.

She could count on one hand the amount of times she and Gerard had lain together—none of them pleasant, so she was glad the number was low. It wasn't like that for every couple? It couldn't be. If it were, she couldn't imagine a woman ever being happy with her husband. But she had seen, and known, lots of couples that were happy with each other.

Couples that were blissfully in love.

She wanted that kind of love.

She slipped her dress off and let the material pool on the floor. In her trunk were the nightdresses she'd purchased from the modiste. Some much too revealing. Others more modest. She chose one of the modest ones that offered the most coverage and slipped it over her head. Then she removed her stockings and crawled on the mattress, drawing the covers up to her chin. Once she was settled, she called out to Finlay.

"Are ye settled?" he asked, still facing the fire.

"Aye," she whispered, watching as he turned and his gaze settled on her, his face softening.

Finishing his wine, he tugged at the buttons of his shirt as he approached the bed. Stopping on her side of the bed, he smiled down at her, before bending and placing the lightest of kisses on her cheek. He didn't say a word as he straightened and walked over to his side of the bed and sat down to tug off his boots.

Next, he pulled his shirt over his head. She tried to drag her eyes away from his back, full of muscles that rippled with every movement.

She should be affording him the same amount of privacy that he had her. But she couldn't. Instead, she found her mouth dry. She swallowed. Hard. Biting her lip as she continued to stare.

When he unbuttoned his trousers and pulled them down, baring his buttocks, she had to bite back a gasp. Powerful, muscled buttocks and thighs treated her eyes to a divine feast.

Her husband was a verra fine specimen. Before he slipped between the covers, he snuffed the candle, and then the bed shifted under his weight.

The barrier of pillows she'd set up earlier still allowed them plenty of room so that didn't make her feel guilty doing it. Though she did feel a wee bit of guilt for insisting on it in the first place. At the time it had seemed like a good idea.

Now? She wasn't so sure. What would it feel like to fall asleep wrapped in her husband's arms?

"Mina?" Finlay said softly in the dark.

"Aye?" she whispered.

"I bid ye a good night and thank ye for letting me sleep in the bed."

What could she say to such a statement? It sounded absurd when he voiced it. So she answered with the only thing she could say. "Ye're welcome."

As the minutes wore on, she found sleep eluded her. Finlay's breath evened out and soon, he was softly snoring. Her eyes had adjusted to the dark and she could see him with the help of the light from the fire.

He looked so relaxed as he slept. His features softened. She moved to lay on her side, her hands tucked under her cheek and watched him sleep, fighting the urge to reach out and stroke his hair, his jaw. To splay her hands on his broad chest.

She squeezed her eyes shut. If she kept staring she would never fall asleep. But his image was seared into her lids.

At some point, she must have fallen asleep, because when she next opened her eyes, light filtered through slits of the drapes covering the large windows. She was laying on her back, the covers still up to her neck. She looked to her left, but the other side of the bed was empty. Finlay must have woken earlier and left.

The door opened and she sat up, dragging the covers with her.

Finlay gave her a warm smile from the doorway as he entered. "Good morn, sleepy-head."

She rubbed at her eyes. What time was it? She wasn't usually one to sleep in. "Good morn." She watched him as he walked about the room before grabbing the poker and jabbing at the remnants of the logs that had burned through the night. Embers flew and he added another log from the rack nearby.

"I thought ye might be hungry, so Cook is making something

to break your fast and will send it up when 'tis ready."

"Have ye eaten yet?"

"Nay. Just a cup of tea. I thought we could break our fast together."

"I would verra much like that."

He smiled and slapped his knee as he straightened. "Perfect." He went to the windows and pulled open the drapes, securing them in the hooks on each side of the pane. There were three large windows in this room. In front of the middle one, a round table with two chairs was set up. "We can eat here if ye like?"

She realized she still sat with the covers pulled up and flushed. Sensing her distress, he turned and took a sudden intense interest in the grounds below. Understanding what he was doing, she slipped out from the covers and pulled on her robe. It was light blue and thick enough that it covered what she was wearing underneath. She tied the cinch and walked over to Finlay, peering down to see what he was looking at.

It was literally naught. A stone pathway that appeared to loop around the exterior, which was empty.

"Thank ye," she said warmly.

He raised a brow at her. "For?"

"My privacy. E'en though we are closed together in this room, ye have allowed me privacy and I verra much appreciate it."

He smiled. "Whate'er I can do to make ye feel comfortable, I shall strive to do so." A soft knock sounded. "Ah, that should be our meal." He left the window to fetch the tray and she took a seat.

She watched his confident strides as he approached the table, setting the tray down and moving the items so he could divest of the tray.

"Let us see what Cook has served up for us." He took the cover off one dish to reveal toast. Under another was eggs. The last one held pork. "What would you like?"

The smells filling the room were like heaven to Willamina's

senses and her stomach answered with a loud growl. Embarrassed, she clutched at her stomach.

He lifted a brow. "I ken that means ye are verra hungry and would like at least one of e'erything." Filling a plate with more food than she could possibly eat, he set it down in front of her and then poured her a cup of tea, adding two sugar cubes and a splash of milk, just as she liked.

The small gesture that showed her he had been paying attention when they had dined together previously warmed her heart, and had the veil that she viewed him through lifting.

With his own plate filled, he sat back and studied her.

She felt her skin flush under the scrutiny. Then she remembered she was in her robe and had not brushed her hair and probably looked a mess.

"Ye look beautiful," he said, reading her mind.

Not knowing how to react, she picked up her tea cup and took a long sip.

"I was thinking that since we are practically mandated to our chamber for the next few days at the verra least, that we could spend some time getting to ken each other better."

Of all the things she expected Finlay to say, that was not one of them at all. But also her nerves jumped into her throat. She cleared her throat and tilted her head before meeting his eyes. "What would ye like to ken?"

"Why did your cousin insist ye leave Inverness when ye love it so much?"

Well, if that didn't get right to the point, she did not ken what would. "'Tis complicated." She took a bite of toast, chewing slowly.

"How so? Your old friends at the theater gave me a glimpse, but no' enough to understand the gravity of what happened. And something most certainly happened. Ye ken my secret. 'Tis time to reveal yours."

He took a sip of tea and looked at her expectantly.

When she didn't speak up, he continued to talk. "Ye seem to

long to go back e'en though something clearly happened there aside from your marriage. I thought that now that we are married, we could make the trip."

"What?" Her brows rose in shock. She would like naught more than to return to the city she grew up in. Where all her memories were made. Both good and bad. But did she dare? She was unsure what their reception would be once people learned she was back, especially after seeing Clarice and Viola. "I am no' so sure that is the best of ideas."

"Did something happen there? Other than your husband? Your cousin eluded to some controversy but didna expound any further."

"Did he?"

Finlay nodded. "And we canna forget your friends that we met the other night."

This was the time where she would find out if Finlay would think her daft. But with naught else to lose, what could it hurt to ask his opinions? "Do ye believe that we can speak to the dead, Finlay?"

He choked on the bite of eggs he had just taken. Coughing and catching his breath, he dabbed at the corners of his mouth with the napkin. "Excuse me?"

She pressed her lips together and met his eyes. "When people pass, do ye believe that some people, no' all, can speak to them?" she asked seriously.

He lifted his hand a couple of times before rubbing his nose and wetting his lips. "I havena e'er really thought of such things."

"But if ye did, do ye think 'tis possible?"

He waved his hands in the air. "I suppose. I have heard of people in the past that claimed to do as such, but I ne'er paid them much attention."

She took another bite of toast, chewing slowly as she bid her time to continue. "I, when I was in Inverness, after my husband died, I would hold parties at my home."

"I see no issue with doing such a thing."

"They werena your usual party. They were seances."

She let the word hang in the air and watched Finlay's forehead crease in confusion. "I dinna understand."

"My friends and I would gather at my house. I had made the acquaintance of a reputable medium—one that can speak with the dead."

"This was something that ye and your friends all participated in?"

She nodded. "Until the last party. I went with another medium, who in the end was a fraud. She said awful things to my friends that supposedly had come from their loved ones. Made an awful show of trying to make it seem like she was being overcome by spirits. Speaking in tongues. It was horrifying. My friends cried foul and blamed me for the fraudulent woman's actions."

"But hadna ye already provided them with someone reputable?"

"I had, but it didna matter. Word spread like wildfire in Inverness, and my friends abandoned me. The city shunned me. I was alone. And with my parents gone I had no one left."

He sat back in his chair, staring out the window at the clouds hanging low in the autumn sky.

Would he put her out? Send her away? Ask for annulment? She wrung her hands together in her lap as she worried her lower lip with her teeth. They certainly had not consummated their marriage. He was well within his rights to demand such a thing.

"Mina, I can honestly say that I have no experience in such a thing. Was it something ye found helpful? Who did ye speak with?"

She shook her head. "'Twas ne'er for myself. I had no one I wanted to connect with. E'en after Gerard died, I didna want to see if the medium could contact him, though she did tell me once that e'en if I wanted to, I couldna. She wasna able to see his spirit at all. I had closed that chapter in my life and moved forward. But my friends? They wanted to speak with old friends, parents, siblings, children they'd lost. I just found the whole thing fascinating and since I had the means, I hosted."

She clasped her hands together so tightly her knuckles were white. "I understand if ye would like to release yourself from me."

"What? Why would ye say such a thing?"

She shrugged. "I just, since I," she stammered, not able to come up with a coherent sentence.

"The fact that ye made a mistake and your friends decided to turn their backs on ye, doesna change my mind. I ken naught of how seances work, but I also think if ye mentioned it to my friends' wives, they would have their interest piqued."

Her eyes rounded. Finlay's reaction was the opposite of what she had expected. Her cousin told her she needed her head examined for finding interest in such a morbid topic. But not Finlay.

"I think your friends were no' your friends for abandoning ye in such a way." He stood up and paced the length of the room until he stopped suddenly and pointed a finger in the air. "I believe we should honeymoon in Inverness," he stated.

Willamina's eyes snapped to his, her head shaking from side to side. "Surely, ye canna mean that."

He leaned on the table in front of her, their eyes at the same level and smiled. "I do. One should ne'er be run out of the home they loved for such a trivial thing. Let us show Inverness that Willamina Primrose is back."

FINLAY WAS TAKEN aback at Willamina's reaction to returning to Inverness. Her main reason for their marriage was so that she could regain control of her assets.

The busy bitties that she called friends obviously lived more for gossip and scandal than actual friendship. How dare they practically run Willamina out of town.

"We shall leave in the morning."

Her eyes fell to her trunk. "I suppose 'tis good that I didna unpack my things then." She took a sip of tea and sighed. "This isna necessary, Finlay. I am sure out of all of your travels, ye can think of other places of which ye would like to spend a holiday."

He shrugged. "It makes no matter. Ye dinna want your estate to stay unmanaged for too long." He placed his hand on hers and smiled when she didn't pull away from his touch. "Besides, I want to see how ye lived up there in the highlands."

"'Tis getting late in the year. The weather will be cold."

"Then we shall pack accordingly."

She still looked uncertain.

"Willamina. Trust me. We will have a most enjoyable honeymoon there. And ye will be away from the prying eyes of e'eryone here making certain we are honeymooning properly." He winked at her and she laughed. A true laugh. One he hadn't heard in a while.

"'Tis settled then. How do ye like your food? If there is something no' to your liking, I will speak with Cook."

Shaking her head, she took another bite of eggs, chewing before she answered him. "That willna be necessary. In fact, I'm afraid ye will be sorely disappointed with my Cook. Yours puts her to shame. But dinna tell her I said such so," she giggled and dabbed at her mouth.

"I do have some business to attend. E'en though we are honeymooning." He finished his tea. "'Tis with my father's solicitor if ye would like to join me?"

"I think I shall stay here and get ready for our journey."

He nodded, not the least surprised that she didn't want to come with him for the meeting. He had to sign paperwork showing that he had indeed married before his birthday and would be retaining the title. Much to his brother's chagrin, but, truly, Fingal should have known better.

An hour later, he and Fingal were sitting in the study of their father's longtime solicitor Bernard Bigsby. Fingal hadn't stopped glaring at him since he'd arrived and slouched in the chair beside his.

"Well," Bigsby said, as he pored over the papers spread across his desk. "It appears all is in order. Your father's demands have been met and no further actions are needed. Congratulations on your marriage, Lord Primrose."

"Pfft," Fingal grunted. "He doesna e'en love the chit."

"I suggest ye watch your tongue, brother, and show some respect to my *wife*," Finlay warned.

"Most marriages doona start with love," Bigsby stated matter-of-factly. "Your father had no such requirement. Only that the marriage must take place before your twenty-eighth birthday. That has been followed. There is naught further to do."

Fingal just shook his head and seethed quietly. "This is such a farce. Who puts such a thing in their damned will?"

Finlay pinched the bridge of his nose. He was tired of the same old argument, over and over again. "Might I remind ye, that e'en if father had no' written such a clause, ye still wouldna get the title on our birthday."

"Nay, ye dinna. But barring your death, this was my one chance."

Finlay couldn't believe his ears. His brother really was that selfish. The bastard. "Well, I believe we are done here and I must get back to my wife. We are readying to travel to Inverness in the morn." He stood and stuck out his hand for a shake. "Thank ye, Bigsby. 'Twas nice seeing ye again." He stuck his hat on his head, and pinched the brim as he said his goodbyes to his brother.

As he left the room, he could hear Fingal continue to complain. He felt for the lawyer. The poor man was going to have to listen to Fingal for Lord knew how much longer until he finally tired and gave up.

His brother would get over the reality eventually. He wouldn't be surprised if he set Yvette aside and went back to whoring his way through Edinburgh. Whatever his brother decided to do, Finlay needn't worry about it. Nor did he plan on thinking about him while he was spending time in Inverness.

On his honeymoon.

The trip would take him and Willamina two days if they pushed it. They'd stop at an inn for the night on the morrow and to switch out the horses.

Happy to return to his wife, he left Bigsby's house. Knowing that their union was only on paper didn't dissuade him from hoping for something more. He'd be lying if he hoped that their Inverness trip would allow Willamina to finally realize that she deserved love. Her late husband was a shite. He wanted her to see that marriage didn't need to be miserable. She deserved respect.

Hell, she deserved to be put on a pedestal and worshipped.

He shook his head. For someone who didn't want to get married, he sure did find himself pining after his fake wife.

CHAPTER SIXTEEN

THE DAY HAD dragged on while Willamina and Finlay were confined to the carriage. The road to Inverness was long and extremely bumpy. Her bottom was sore and by the time their carriage stopped and she was able to get out and stretch her legs, she nearly broke down in tears from the relief.

Beside her Finlay held back a chuckle at her plight. "I shall see to a pillow for ye to sit upon for the ride on the morrow," he jested.

She rolled her eyes as she took the arm he offered and they entered the inn. "I dinna recall the ride to Edinburgh to be so uncomfortable, but I had much on my mind to keep me thinking of other things. I also stopped more often. I didna feel like hastening my arrival," she confessed.

"I can understand that. Mayhap I shouldna have pushed so much today. I thought only one night on the road would be better than multiple."

"'Tis fine." She let go of Finlay's arm while he checked them in and took the time to look around the cozy entry. The wood floors were covered in woven rugs and the walls were papered in blue and gold birds. Off to the right, there appeared to be a dining room. To the left, a set of stairs that she assumed would lead them to their room.

"Welcome, my lord, lady. If ye will follow me I shall show ye to your room," the man behind the desk snapped his fingers and a footman rushed forward, picked up their overnight bags, and waited for them to ascend the stairs before him.

"I have saved a corner room for ye, my lord. 'Tis out of the way and should be quiet for ye both. Dinner will be served in a few hours if ye are hungry." He inserted the key into the lock and twisted, then pushed the door open and stepped aside. "I have taken the initiative to have wine brought in and set up." He gestured to a table containing the decanter and glasses. "If ye require anything else, please call for me." The man bowed and once the porter set down their bags, they left the room, shutting the door behind them.

Willamina studied the large bed. It wasn't as large as the bed they had at Rosewood Manor, but it appeared to be big enough that she could still set up some type of barrier to separate them.

As if reading her mind, Finlay walked over to her and tipped her on the nose. "Ye ken, I can control myself without whatever barrier ye construct betwixt us." He gave her a smile and went to pour himself a glass of wine. "Would ye like one?"

"Please." Barrier forgotten for now, she joined him at the square mahogany table set in the corner, though she remained standing. "We have been stuck sitting for so long, I just want to stretch my legs." She sipped from her glass; the wine was good, even if it was on the slightly bitter side. There was one window in the room and she made her way over to it to gaze outside.

Below them, the street bustled with life. A constant stream of people walked by and she was thankful that they were not on the first floor. Not that they couldn't close the drapes, they could, of course, but she liked seeing outside.

"Are ye nervous about returning home?"

She pressed her lips together. Was nervous the right word? Nay. "I canna say nervous. Trepidatious, mayhap? I wonder how I will be received once word gets out that I have returned." As much as she loved Inverness, and as miserable she was when she'd left, she still hadn't wanted to leave.

She would be happy, holed up in Warton House, whilst she tried to ignore the world going on around her. It wouldn't take long for people to realize she had come back. Or that she was remarried. Especially if Clarice or Viola returned before she and Finlay arrived. And since her husband was someone of influence, higher in title than her late husband, she expected some of her old *friends* to trip over themselves trying to get back in her good graces. But she had no intentions of falling for that. If they could leave her when she was her most vulnerable, then they were no friends of hers.

Just as Finlay had told her. Funny how she could see it now. Back when they'd abandoned her, she had been too hurt to see it as anything other than a failure on her part.

The snobbiness of society and how people could turn from loving you to shunning you on the turn of a pence was tiring. It was not something she enjoyed, so she was in no rush to enter back into it.

"I always found it amazing how fast news made its way around the city," he quipped. "'Twas as if there were messenger pigeons on each windowsill, just waiting and ready to send the news along to whoe'er was interested."

She nodded. Too many times she had been the topic of such gossip. She didn't want to be thrust into that position again.

Finlay clasped his hands together. "Shall we get ready for dinner?"

After they had filled their bellies with some delicious food, they had returned to their room and Willamina was faced with the same dilemma she thought about earlier.

Barrier or no barrier?

She trusted Finlay, wholeheartedly. But the longer they stayed together, the more she lost trust in herself.

As she dressed for bed, Finlay took up his usual position of staring into the flames of the fire until she was under the covers, and she told him she was ready.

His smile lit up the room when he saw that she hadn't con-structed a wall to separate them. But he didn't say anything about it. Just walked to his side of the bed and kicked off his boots before unbuttoning his trousers and sliding them down his hips, baring his buttocks to her.

She enjoyed this nightly ritual. Mayhap more than she should. She was sure that he knew she watched him, but he never said anything to her. He slipped his shirt over his head, the light playing off the planes of his muscles, and then snuffed the candle before slipping into bed.

And every night, she listened to his breathing even out and slow. He fell asleep so easily. She was a bit jealous of that. She had never been much of a sleeper. But it allowed her to watch him all the while fighting the urge to reach out and stroke his strong jaw. To push her hands through his hair.

She sighed, settling into her pillow, wondering how long she would be able to fight her feelings for her husband.

NIGHT HAD FALLEN when they finally arrived at Warton House. Candles lit the windows and the house seemed to be alive. It didn't appear to be abandoned as Willamina worried. Gil must have ensured that the staff stayed on board while she was away.

Or, he had hired them back once she wed and learned she would be returning.

Finlay noticed her breathing had quickened the closer they got to her estate.

With a hand on her knee, Finlay leaned in and whispered, "Relax. No one kens ye are back yet. All will be well."

She nodded and gave him a small smile before wringing her hands in her lap once again. "The house does appear to be awaiting our arrival."

He patted her leg. "Indeed it does. Shall we?"

Her eyes darted back and forth between the house, the interior of the carriage and Finlay. As he waited for her to prepare herself for her return, he studied the house. Taking in what he could see in the torchlit yard.

It was built of gray stone, and appeared to be three stories. The outside was rather plain with two steps leading to the front door, which was painted red. No other real discerning designs were apparent. Mayhap he would see more in the light of day.

Willamina took a deep breath and blew it out slowly through her teeth. "I believe I am ready."

He pushed the door of the carriage open and exited before turning and offering her his hand for assistance.

Her eyes swept the house, and her hesitancy rolled off her body in waves. Finlay understood that. From everything she had previously said, any happy memories she may have had here were far and few between. It was one of the reasons he insisted they come—to replace the bad with the good. No one should harbor hard feelings perpetually. They had a way of eating one up from the inside out. 'Twas not a healthy way to live.

He bent to her and whispered in her ear encouragingly, "Take all the time ye need. I'm here." Whether his presence offered her any solace, he knew not, but he hoped so.

As eager as he was to get off the street and inside the house, Willamina was not. He studied her face. The plethora of emotions playing across it was heartbreaking and for a moment he wondered if he'd made a mistake in insisting that they honeymoon here.

With a final heave of breath, she squared her shoulders, jutted out her chin, and moved forward. She paused at the door before turning the knob and walking inside, and he followed on her heels.

The entry was high-ceilinged and bright. An older man rushed forward from one of the back rooms to greet her. "My lady," he looked over his shoulder up the stairs, concern creasing his already wrinkled brow, surprise making his eyes wide. "We werena expecting ye this eve."

"Aye, Harold. Good eve. I apologize for not sending advance notice. We planned this visit at the last moment." She paused, and then her cheeks flushed. "Och, my manners. Harold, please meet my husband, Finlay Primrose, Earl of Rosebery."

"My lord," the butler dipped his head in greeting.

"I am sure ye need some time to freshen things up at such late notice, so Finlay and I shall wait in the parlor. If you could have Mrs. Fitz bring tea and whatever might be available to eat. 'Tis been a long journey and an e'en longer day."

"My lady, er," Harold looked nervously toward the stairs again.

Finlay got the feeling that something wasn't right. He narrowed his eyes as he assessed the butler. Mayhap he was the only staff on hand. "Harold, if ye are alone, we can make the tea. 'Tis no issue."

"Nay, my lord." The poor man looked a tinge green in the collar.

Finlay narrowed his eyes. "Whate'er is the issue, then?" he asked, genuinely curious as to what was happening. "Do ye require more time to ready the room?"

"N-nay."

Finlay was beginning to think that the butler suffered from some type of affliction that prevented him from speaking any words other than nay suddenly.

"Then what is it?"

Willamina had cocked her head to the side as she studied her butler. "Truly, Harold. What seems to be the issue?"

The man cleared his throat, clearly uncomfortable. "I am afraid that I canna ready your room at this time, my lady."

Willamina nodded as if she understood. "'Tis of the late hour. I understand."

"I dinna think ye do, my lady. Ye see—"

"Harold!" A male voice called from above. "What is this ruckus that I am hearing?"

Willamina stiffened at his side, her eyes wide in shock, her face suddenly void of all color.

"Mina?" he put his arm around her shoulders to steady her as she began to sway for fear she may faint.

A man in a night robe appeared at the top of the stairs, his hands on his hips. "What the hell is going on down there, Harold?"

"Gerard," Willamina gasped, and went limp in his arms.

Gerard? As in her husband? Her *dead* husband?

CHAPTER SEVENTEEN

WILLAMINA HEARD HER name being called from afar, as if the caller was in a distant tunnel.

"Mina," Finlay called, his voice, laced with concern, was closer, clearer.

Opening her eyes, she saw his face above hers, his brow furrowed. "Mina," he said with a sigh of relief.

She looked around, and realized she was on the chaise in the salon of Warton House. Trying to sit up, she pushed off her elbows, but Finlay's hands were firm on her shoulders, keeping her down. "What happened?"

Finlay's eyes softened. "Ye took a wee break for a faint," he answered, trying to make light of the situation.

"Why d—" The question died on her lips as the events from earlier rushed back to her. She pushed Finlay's hands off her and sat up. "Gerard. He is alive?" She asked. "I-I dinna understand. He-he died."

Finlay shrugged. "I dinna have any answers for ye, lass. I have barred him from coming into this room. When ye are ready, we can work on getting the answers that ye seek. Here," he shoved a glass of whisky in her hands. "Drink this."

He did not have to tell her twice. She drank the amber liquid in one swallow, hissing as it made a burning path down her throat and into her chest.

Confusion muddled her brain. How was it possible? She had been told he had died. His body had never been recovered from the sea, but she had been told that was common. They'd had his funeral. She'd done her mourning period.

Someone pounded on the door and Finlay rushed to it, swinging it open. "What do ye want, Watson?" He growled, and Willamina found herself smiling at his defensiveness.

"Ye canna speak to me that way. I would watch your tongue if I were ye," Gerard snapped back.

Finlay planted his feet and crossed his arms as he glared at her husband. But, Finlay was her husband.

Oh God. She put her hand up to her forehead. She had two husbands. Did that make her a bigamist? Her breath quickened. What was she going to do?

"Ye need to step back. When Willamina is ready, and if, *if*, she wants to speak with ye, then we can have a conversation. Until then, ye would be wise to get the hell out of my sight."

Finlay moved to close the door.

"She's my wife."

As fast as lightning, Finlay spun around and poked his finger into Gerard's chest. Hard. Hard enough to push him back. "Nay," he sneered. "She is *my* wife. She ceased to be yours upon your supposed death."

Willamina fanned herself. The room was suddenly too hot even though the fire remained unlit. Her breaths were still coming in quick succession and she couldn't get them to slow.

Finlay slammed the door and joined her on the chaise lounge, pulling her into his arms and hugging her close.

She couldn't help it. Deep, wracking sobs broke from somewhere deep within her chest, and she buried her face in the lapels of his jacket.

He said nothing as his hands stroked up and down her back in a soothing motion.

She felt safe. Cared for. Dare she say *loved*?

Never had anyone stood up for her like Finlay just had.

Not her parents. Her friends. And certainly not her formerly dead former husband.

But he wasn't her former husband now, was he? Och, she was so confused.

She choked out another sob, swiping at her eyes as she pulled away from the warmth and solace that Finlay offered.

She met his eyes, the usual ice-blue dark with concern.

"I dinna ken what to do. What happens now?" She spat, anger replacing the sorrow she was feeling just moments ago.

She pushed up from the chaise and began to pace the floor a few lengths, before turning back to Finlay. "He was dead. *Dead!*" She all but screamed, frustration getting the best of her. All of their plans. All of their ideas for how they would handle the future were thrown out with the bath water.

Aye, their marriage wasn't real. But it was starting to feel that way. Now, their union truly wasn't real. How could it be? Gerard still being alive would surely make any vows agreed upon between her and Finlay null and void.

She was devastated. Not because she wouldn't gain control of her assets. Her assets be damned. She was devastated because her marriage truly wasn't a marriage. Just when she had finally begun to accept the feelings that were starting to take hold for Finlay, it was all going to be ripped away from her.

Another thought entered her mind and she couldn't stop the gasp that escaped from her. What of Finlay's title? If they werena truly married, then he would no longer be earl. He would be ruined.

All because of her.

"I need to speak with him," she started to the door, but Finlay reached out, stopping her with his hand on her wrist.

"I dinna think ye should rush out there. Think about what ye want to ask him."

"Damn it, I want answers. I think I deserve that. I'm owed an answer as to why."

Finlay pressed his lips together and nodded, letting go of her wrist. "I understand and I agree. He owes ye that much at the verra least after what ye've been through. I just want ye to ensure that this is a conversation ye want to have this night."

Her eyes fell on the door before meeting his once again. "'Tis no' a conversation I would like to have—now or e'er really. But I must ken why." She couldn't explain the pull to Finlay. Her thoughts were a jumbled mess inside her head. But one thing was clear. She wanted answers.

Finlay must have realized that he wouldn't be able to dissuade her from confronting her bastard of a husband until a later time, so he opened the door and followed her out into the hall. "I am here, Mina. Whate'er ye need from me. Just say the word and 'tis yours."

She turned to him and did the one thing she had been dreaming about since before their wedding day—she wound her arms around his neck and pulled his head down for a kiss. A deep, soul-searching, earth-shattering kiss that had her toes curling in her travel boots. As his tongue found hers, her knees went weak, and if it were not for his arms wrapped around her waist holding her steady, she would have collapsed into a puddle on the floor.

Breaking the kiss, she licked her lips, and gave him a shy smile, the complete opposite of his which looked positively feral. His blue eyes burned hot and if it weren't for the pressing matter of questioning her previously dead husband, she would have grabbed Finlay's hand and pulled him into her bedchamber and happily given herself to him.

She drew a shaky breath and smoothed her skirts.

"Let us go talk to my husband."

"Hey," he caught her chin and forced her face to his. "Look at me," he demanded. When her eyes clashed with his, he said. "I am your husband. Me," he clasped her hand and brought it hard against his chest where his heart beat strong beneath her palm. "Only me. That bastard in there? We will figure it out. But it doesna change the fact that *I* am your husband."

FINLAY SPOKE WITH such raw honesty that she could only nod in agreement.

"Say it," he commanded. "I want to hear ye say it."

She took a deep, shuddering breath and met his eyes. "Ye are my husband." The way her heart swelled when she whispered the words was unlike anything she had ever felt before. She smiled and the smile he gave her in return lit up the hall.

"Now, let's go find that bastard and get to the bottom of whate'er game 'tis he is playing." He offered her his arm and when she took it, he said, "Lead the way, *wife*."

She couldn't suppress the laugh that bubbled up, but quickly covered it up and put on a serious face. It would do her no good to confront Gerard in a light manner. When they were married and he treated her like muck on the bottom of his boot, she may have allowed it. But, since she'd met Finlay, she'd gained a new confidence in herself. He made her feel like she was someone.

They found Gerard in the library, a most peculiar place seeing how he had never much cared for the room or the books contained within.

"Willamina," he stood when they entered the room, but she stopped whatever he was going to say by putting her hand up in the air.

"Ye can sit, Gerard," she said, clasping her hands in front of her, trying to decide how best to broach whatever it was that brought them to this point. Deciding the best way would be to get straight to the point, she asked, "Why?"

Gerard had the audacity to look shocked by her question. "Does it matter now, love? Ye are home." He went to stand and Finlay jumped toward him.

"I suggest ye sit your arse in that chair and no' fucking move it."

Willamina dipped her head to hide her smile as she approached Finlay and, with a hand on her chest, gave him a slight shake of her head. She wanted to handle this on her own. Nay, she needed to handle this on her own.

She spun on Gerard. "First, dinna call me love. Ye ne'er did afore when we were married, and ye may no' do so now. Second, I am home. This home is mine. As so granted upon your death."

Gerard clucked his tongue and wagged his index finger at her, a sneer on his face. "See, that 'tis where ye are wrong. The estate went to your parents upon my death." He held up his hands to make the sign of quotes when he said the word death. "Then they died. Sorry," he said flatly, his voice lacking any sign of caring.

"Then, who knew ye had family outside of your parents? I fully expected the estate to go back to the state since ye couldna be the holder."

Her eyes narrowed. "What are ye saying? Ye faked your death so ye could wait for who knew how long and have the estate turned back o'er to ye?" She shook her head, not understanding his reasoning. "Ye had no idea how long that would be. Didna ken my parents would—" The sentence died on her lips as a morbid thought entered her mind. "Did ye kill my parents to regain your estate?" She couldn't help the rise of her voice. Her parents didn't treat her the best, and were always more worried about themselves than her, but she would never wish them ill will.

"Watch your tongue, Willamina. That is a serious accusation ye make."

Her hands fisted at her side. "Did ye?"

"Nay, but their," he paused and smirked, "untimely deaths did help move things along."

"Ye are a bastard."

He raised a brow in surprise. "It appears meek, little Willamina has found her voice while I have been away."

"Away? E'eryone thought ye were dead!"

He shrugged. "Right. But, alas, here I am." He held his arms out as if saying 'look at me, I'm right here'. Standing, he put his hands up to stop Finlay's advance. "Easy. I've no plans to touch her. Or ye, for that matter."

"Why the ruse, then? None of this makes any sense to me."

His eyes slammed into hers. "Would ye be mad if I said I liked watching ye suffer?"

With the speed of lightning, Finlay had Gerard on the floor, his fists connecting with Gerard's face over and over again.

She screamed for him to stop. Pulled at his shoulders. Tried catching his fists. Not because she cared for Gerard. Nay. It was Finlay. He was who she fashed over. "Finlay!" She yelled one last time and finally broke through the all-encompassing rage pulsing through him.

He pushed off Gerard and stood, cranking his head from side to side as he reached for his handkerchief to wipe his hands.

From the floor, Gerard laughed as he sat up. He turned his head and spit blood. "Punch me all ye want, ye prick, at the end of the day, she is still my wife."

Willamina couldn't take any more. She pulled at Finlay's arm. "Let's go."

"Where?"

She shrugged. "I dinna ken, but we canna stay here."

They left the library, but not before Gerard got in the last word. "Ye can leave for the night, wife. But I expect your arse to be here first thing in the morning."

It took all of her strength to stop Finlay from running back into the library and finishing what he had started.

As they were leaving, she noticed a figure on the stairs and for the second time that night, she was shocked at what she saw.

There, looking at her with an evil smile on her face, arms crossed in front of her, stood the woman responsible for getting Willamina run out of Inverness.

Lady Esmerelda.

The fake medium that ruined her. She was working with Gerard?

Did she and Gerard both work together to ruin her?

Her sinister laughter echoed in the hallway as Willamina walked outside and slammed the door behind her.

CHAPTER EIGHTEEN

FINLAY'S KNUCKLES WERE sore, and he fully expected them to be swollen and bruised in the morn as they waited for the carriage to come around. He cared naught. The pain was worth it to beat that worthless excuse of a man to a pulp. He would have continued, too, if it weren't for Willamina stopping him.

The louse deserved so much more.

Willamina had his handkerchief and was gently dabbing at the cuts. "We need water to clean these. There is an inn not too far from here that we can room for the night. I can clean them there."

"Come here," he took control of his hands and opened his arms for her to walk into them. "Dinna fash about me. How do ye fare?"

She did as he wanted and he wrapped his arms around her as her arms snaked around his waist, and laid her cheek against his chest. He rested his chin on the top of her head while he waited for her to answer.

Her deep inhale told him more than her words ever could. The universe had opened to her this night and turned her world upside down. Things she had thought were set were not.

Her arsehole of a husband had risen from the dead. He had even hinted about her parents' deaths. Finlay didn't think he really had anything to do with them, but he would request an investigation into the matter and the circumstances surrounding their carriage accident.

"I dinna ken how I am feeling right now. There are so many things running through my head. It still doesna make sense to me. I just dinna ken what he would gain from such a ruse?"

"I, too, am uncertain." The sod clearly did not want to be married to Willamina. He had never treated her with any respect. Not once from the day they were married. So, this whole scheme seemed absolutely unnecessary.

Their carriage pulled up and he helped her inside before climbing in and sitting beside her.

"You tell me where and we will go."

He relayed her directions to their coachman and the carriage jolted forward, the wheels rambling along the cobblestone road.

Her face was solemn as she looked through the window at the houses they passed. Were they the homes of her former friends? Quite possibly so, he assumed. He wondered what was going through her mind—other than the obvious.

They rode in silence. Tension rolled off her in waves, filling the cabin of the carriage. That, he could understand. If he had just been confronted with such news, he would probably be feeling the same way. He couldn't fault her.

Instead, he put his arm around her shoulders and pulled her in close. If anything, he wanted to show her that he was here. He wasn't going anywhere. It didn't matter what her former husband—he refused to call the bastard her husband—said or did. It wouldn't change the way he felt about her. Willamina might still not see it, but he still held out hope that she would eventually.

There was a spark there. He knew she felt that much. She solidified it when she initiated that scorching kiss in the hallway before confronting Gerard.

The passion she put forth in that kiss, that was real. One couldn't fake that reaction.

The carriage slowed before pulling to a stop in front of a three-story brick mansion, with white trim. "This the place ye mentioned?"

She lifted her head and nodded.

They entered through the door, also painted white, their coachman behind them, their overnight bags in his hands.

After securing a room for the night, Finlay requested food, tea, and wine be brought to their room, and gave the innkeeper two extra shillings for his efforts. The man nodded, a huge smile suddenly plastered on his face.

They made their way to the third floor and unlocked the door to their room. He looked around. 'Twas nice enough and would suit them for the night. A fireplace encased in brick to match the outside of the house was centered in the wall to their right. Beside it, a crate held a pile of logs and a steel poker leaned against the wall. Two chairs adorned with red cushions along with a small table between them were set in front. Two large windows with red drapes took up most of the space of one wall with a small dresser between them. A good sized bed with a plush red duvet that matched the drapes and cushions was on the other wall. Two small tables on either side. Perfectly suitable.

In the morn, they would figure out how they would move forward.

He was perfectly fine with returning to Edinburgh. He had enough estates and coin to ensure Willamina was well cared for. He didn't need Warton House. He understood that she wanted it. It was her sense of security. But he could offer her the same, without all the heartache that would come with trying to reclaim her home.

With Gerard alive, it would be a fight that she would more than likely lose. Though if she did want to fight for it, he would support her wholeheartedly.

"'Tis been a long day. I already requested sustenance, but I feel a bath is in order after the day we have had? What do ye think?"

She stood in the center of the room, worrying her bottom lip between her teeth. A habit of hers that he found far too enticing. "A bath would be nice, indeed."

"I will leave so ye may bathe in peace."

She bounced from one foot to the other. "Ye needna do so," she said quietly, looking at him through lowered lashes.

Now if that didn't shoot a signal straight to his cock. She was inviting him to stay while she bathed? This was progress indeed. Not wanting to scare her with his eagerness, he nodded. "I will have two baths brought up."

This time, her eyes locked with his and she shook her head. "I dinna think there is need for two," her voice had turned sultry and his senses fired off all at once.

He cleared his throat, and nodded stiffly. "Are ye certain?" he asked.

She nodded confidently. "I have ne'er been more so."

WILLAMINA KNEW WHAT she had to do. And as much as her heart was saying that she needed to stay with Finlay, her mind was telling her what she really needed to do.

Though their marriage was a farce, on paper it would still have been legal. But with Gerard alive and well, it voided any contract they had made.

She wouldn't put Finlay through the scandal that would ensue if she stayed with him. She'd felt the wrath of what a scandal could do to someone and their livelihood. There was no way she would play a part in that happening to Finlay.

But, her heart was selfish.

She would leave, but in the early hours of the morning.

For this night, she was only thinking of herself. When she told Finlay they only needed one bath she meant it.

They drank wine while the tub was being filled with hot water. Her nerves were on edge, and the wine was going down smoothly and quickly. A refill of the decanter was ordered. Finally, she felt her body unwind just a bit. Her nerves settle just a tad.

With the tub filled, the maids left the room, and she and Finlay were once again alone. She bit her bottom lip, thinking of what she should do next. In her mind, she knew what she wanted to happen. If she was going to return to her loveless marriage and be miserable for the rest of her life, she wanted one night.

One night to be cherished. To experience what it felt like to be loved. This night was all about making memories that would last her a lifetime. To get her through what she would have to endure once she returned to Warton House.

Finlay had been watching her, trying to read her expressions. She hoped he couldn't read her thoughts. She didn't want him to know her plans. He would try to stop her, she was certain of it. And that couldn't happen.

Not for him and his future. Without her, he could still marry in time. He would meet another woman to make a marriage pact with and secure his title. She ignored the stab of pain that pierced her heart at the thought of him with another woman.

Because no matter how hard she had tried to fight it, she couldn't.

She was in love with the man that stood before her, looking at her with adoration in his eyes that would be forever emblazoned in her memory.

She finished her wine and gave him what she hoped was a sensual smile. She didn't have experience in such things. As long as she didn't look like a clown, she would be happy.

His beautiful blue eyes, so different from the muddy brown eyes of Gerard, flared and darkened as they clashed with hers.

"I believe the bath is calling our name," she whispered, her voice shaky. It was her first attempt at seduction and she was nervous. But Finlay didn't appear to notice.

"Are ye certain?"

She licked her lips and nodded, tracking his stare as it dropped to her mouth.

His approach was slow, as if he was giving her the option to put a stop to what they were tumbling toward at any time.

When his hands circled her waist and drew her flush against him, she gasped. She could feel him. *All* of him. His hands moved to her face and cupped her jaw, his thumbs feathering over her cheeks as he searched her eyes.

It felt like he was looking into the depths of her soul. She offered no resistance and he must have noticed because his mouth came crashing down on hers, his tongue demanding entry and she melted into him, opening her mouth and savoring the clash of their tongues as they performed a wicked dance. He tasted of the wine they'd consumed earlier. Sweet and tart at the same time, and she sighed.

His hands dropped to her bottom, pushing her against him. She could feel his hardness against her upper belly.

Her fingers moved from the short hair at the nape of his neck to the ties of his shirt, deftly untying them. He watched her movements, his brow furrowed, his eyes intense, his tongue peeking, and wetting his bottom lip as he inhaled sharply.

With the ties released, she pushed the shirt off his broad shoulders. His hands left her bottom and he wriggled out of the arms, letting the linen fall to the floor. She traced the planes of his muscled chest. Trailing them lower, lower, down his abdomen and the muscled ridges there. His sharp intake of breath the only sound in the room other than the crackle of the fire.

He caught her hand and brought it up to his mouth, tenderly kissing her fingers. "Much more of that, lass, and this will end a lot sooner than ye would like." His eyes crinkled with a smile, full of mirth.

Dropping to the floor, he tapped her left foot and she lifted, using his shoulders for balance, his hot skin searing her fingers. He slipped off her boot, then reached up and grasped the lip of her stocking, pulling it down her leg. He paused at her ankle and bent, placing a kiss on the sensitive skin, before slipping the material off her foot. He did the same for her right leg.

He looked up at her from his position sitting at her feet and waggled his eyebrows, causing her to giggle. Pushing off the floor, he stood, dragging his hands up her body, sending shivers from the tips of her toes to the top of her head. His eyes never leaving hers, he slipped her dress off one shoulder, then the next, and she held her breath as he pushed the material down, letting it pool at her feet.

Her cheeks flushed as she stood there before him in naught but her chemise, her chest rising and falling and his eyes, dark with desire, drinking her all in. He dipped his head and his lips scorched a trail from her ear down her neck to her collarbone, feathering little kisses along the way.

Throwing her head to the side, she gave him all the access he wanted, savoring in the feeling that was so foreign to her. His tongue licked his way up her neck and his lips found her mouth once again. As they kissed, he grasped the soft material of her chemise, gathering it up, exposing her legs, then her most private parts, drawing it up further and further, until he had to break the kiss so he could lift it over her head and throw it to the floor.

Cool air caressed her heated skin, and her body shivered. Finlay pulled back and his eyes roamed over her body, a smile of satisfaction breaking out on his face.

She smiled back. "The water will grow cold," she whispered.

"Well, let us no' let it go to waste. Shall we?" He gestured toward the tub, furls of steam still rising from the water. He held out his hand and she accepted it, allowing him to pull her to the basin. Offering his arm to keep her steady as she stepped in, he waited until she was in the water to kick off his own boots.

She waited with bated breath. She had seen him undress multiple times since they'd married, but never once had she seen the front of him. When he pulled his trousers off and faced her, she couldn't stop the smile of pure ecstasy that drew her mouth wide.

Finlay Primrose did not disappoint.

Catching her looking, he laughed as he climbed into the tub behind her, nuzzling her neck. He sat and pulled her down with him, causing water to slosh over the sides.

"We are going to make a mess," she exclaimed.

"Shhh. I shall tip them well in the morning." He nipped at her neck, causing her to shudder.

Washcloth in hand, he dipped it into the water and then dipped the bar of soap under and worked it into the small square of cloth before rubbing it over her back in slow circles. "Give me your arm."

She did as he asked and he held her wrist while he brought the cloth up and down her arm, dipping into her underarm before asking for the other and doing the same. Pulling her back so she rested against his chest, he dipped the cloth once again before bringing it up and letting it drip drops of water on her breasts.

Her breath caught and she sucked her lower lip into her mouth as he brought the cloth to her skin and drew lazy circles of suds around each nipple, drawing them into tight peaks. She blew out her breath on a sigh, and he chuckled close to her ear. "Like that, do ye?"

She nodded, reaching back and snaking her hand around the back of his neck. The feelings he was eliciting in her were erotic and nothing like she had ever felt. She would let this man do whatever he wanted to her.

A touch of sadness entered into her mind when she thought that this night would have to last her a lifetime of memories, but she shook it off. She didn't want to think about the morrow. Only the here and now.

When he dragged the cloth below the water and touched it against her most sensitive area, her hips nearly bucked out of the water. He chuckled again, and said close to her ear "not yet, love" before continuing to bathe her with deft and experienced hands.

"All done," he announced, kissing her neck. And she was glad he hadn't insisted on washing her hair. It was so thick it took forever to dry and she didn't like to go to bed with it wet. Whenever she did, she woke up with it being one big knot that took much too long to brush out. "Grab a linen and dry off. I will wash and join ye momentarily."

She spun around, causing even more water to slosh out of the tub and land on the floor. "I should pay back the favor and wash ye."

He shook his head, his eyes dark. "Nay, lass. I am strung tight as a bow right now. Your fingers on my body will put an end to this much quicker than I want."

She flushed, but nodded, and used his shoulders as balance to get out of the tub. He watched her as she picked up the cloth from the nearby table and wrapped it around herself, patting herself dry.

His eyes followed her every move as he quickly finished bathing. When he stood, her eyes widened. She was pleasantly surprised when he had undressed earlier, but now, he had grown even larger. She didn't think it was possible. But her eyes did not deceive her.

With a moan, she licked her lips. She couldn't help it. Couldn't stop her reaction. Grabbing the other linen, she closed the distance between them and began to pat him down. He threw his head back on a hiss.

"Mina…" he didn't say anything else. Just let her name hang in the air between them. But he didn't let her continue for long. He snatched the cloth from her and quickly dried himself the rest of the way before scooping her up and carrying her over to the bed and laying her down, his body covering hers. "I have had dreams of this."

"What?"

"Aye. From the first night I met ye in the maze, visions of this exact moment have played in my mind."

He kissed her lips. A soft kiss, not one to conquer all her senses, but yet it still had the same effect.

"Just one thing."

When she looked at him questioningly, he reached out for her hair, pulling the pins free and splaying her tresses over the pillow.

"Now this is what I have envisioned. Ye are beautiful, lass."

Quivering beneath him, she flushed. Not knowing what to do with her hands, she brought them up to his shoulders and traced his muscles, watching them contract under her touch.

With a wicked gleam in his eyes, he licked his lips before moving down her body, his tongue circling her taut nipple before tugging it between his teeth.

She gasped at the sensation, unlike anything she had ever felt before. He nipped and then licked away the pain before moving to her other breast and giving it the same attention, his hand kneading the one he'd left, flicking his thumb across the peak.

She shoved her hands in his hair, biting her lip as her core heated in want, jealous of the attention her breasts were receiving. Lifting her hips, trying to hint to him that she wanted him there.

His laugh against her breast caused the most delicious sensation and she called his name. "Fin," she whispered, her voice sounding odd to her own ears.

Lowering himself even further, he swirled his tongue around her navel, and trailed kisses down further, to her damp curls, blowing on them and making her squirm. He hitched her legs on his shoulders and drew his tongue down her slick crease, lapping at her soft folds.

Her hands fisted in his hair, her hips rising to meet every thrust of his tongue, her breaths coming in whimpers.

When he sank his finger between her folds, she gasped. When he added another, and then another, pushing them in and drawing them slowly out, she wanted to cry. The feeling so divine, so all-encompassing, that she thought she would lose her sense of mind. And when he sucked her little bud of pleasure into his mouth, her world shattered into a million pieces. Her body taut, her breath coming in gasps, she saw stars. The universe was exploding around her and Finlay continued to suckle and work his fingers as wave after wave of pleasure washed over her.

Spent, her limbs loosened until they felt like custard. Her

bones were gone. They'd disappeared.

And then Finlay's face was in front of hers, eyes dark with desire, a bright smile plastered on his face. He dipped his head and captured her mouth, and she opened hers, giving his tongue entry. She could taste the tang of herself on his tongue and she deepened the kiss, pulling his head down to hers even more. She wanted to be swallowed up by this man.

His manhood lay heavy on her stomach and she closed her fist around it. Finlay's body jerked in response and he broke the kiss, resting his forehead on hers, panting heavily.

Settling between her thighs, she involuntarily stiffened. This position she was familiar with.

Sensing something was wrong, he pulled back, his eyes imploring hers. "What's wrong?"

She shook her head, refusing to let Gerard taint this memory in any way. Finlay was not Gerard and he would never do anything to hurt her. "'Tis naught." He didn't look convinced, so she brought her lips to his, stroking her hand up and down the hard velvet of his cock.

"Ye shall be the death of me, lass," he whispered when he broke the kiss.

As she gave way to the sensations of feelings she had pulsing through her body, she relaxed.

In one swift move, he entered, taking her breath away. There was no pain, only the exquisite feeling of fullness, and then the feeling of emptiness, longing for more when he pulled away before pushing back inside. He continued that excruciating torture, her senses building and building. Climbing the highest mountain to the peak, and right before she toppled and fell over the cliff, he hastened the pump of his hips, his breath hot in her ear, his pants an erotic song she wanted to listen to for the rest of her life.

And then she fell, floating on air as her limbs stiffened and his name escaped her lips in a cry of passion. He followed suit just moments later, grinding out her name as he ground his hips against her, burying himself as deep as he could, his body spasming right along with hers.

She was having a hard time catching her breath. Coming down from the exquisite journey he had just taken her on. Her chest heaved against his.

"I love ye, lass," Finlay said as he collapsed beside her, dragging her with him so she could rest her head upon his chest.

She couldn't get herself to say the words, even though she knew she loved him, too. If she said them, it would make it that much harder to leave in the morn.

His heart beat a crazy rhythm under her cheek as his fingers drew lazy circles on her back, making her shiver. Reaching down, he pulled the duvet up and covered them.

Tucked into his side, she felt safe. As if no one could break in and ruin their sanctity. If only that were true. But knowing it wasn't, she knew what she had to do. She would be forever thankful to Finlay for these memories. She'd never experienced anything like them, and knew she never would again.

He had no idea how much that meant to her.

The night was still young, and she wasn't ready to stop now. Not now that she knew how pleasurable the act of lovemaking could be. Nay, she'd had a taste and she wanted more. She deserved it after all she had been through.

The universe owed her that much. Owed her all the memories that they would make this night.

Because in the morn she would be gone.

CHAPTER NINETEEN

WILLAMINA AWOKE TO soft kisses trailing along her neck, and warm hands kneading her breasts. Finlay was behind her, his chest flush against her back. His manhood hard against her buttocks.

"I didna mean to wake ye, lass," he whispered into the faint light in the room, and nipped at her ear.

She smiled. "I believe ye fib, sir," she teased and wiggled her bottom, causing him to hiss in her ear. She moved to turn around, but he stopped her.

"Nay, lass. Stay just like that." He maneuvered his body and entered her from behind.

Her breath caught on a gasp. The sensation from this angle completely different than afore. He buried his face into her neck and nuzzled as he thrust into her.

Once she figured out the rhythm, she gyrated her hips, matching his thrust for thrust. His lips moved to her ear, and he grunted with each pump of his strong hips. His arms were locked around her waist, keeping her in place.

That now familiar feeling began to build. Finlay must have sensed it, too, because he spoke in the darkness. "Come on, Mina. Let yourself go. Join me."

He pumped at a hurried pace, and dropped a hand to her nestle of curls, finding that little nub of sensations and applied pleasure as he rubbed it in fast circles.

Her breaths were short, hot. She was climbing that mountain

again. And then his other hand pinched her turgid nipple, and she was gone. Bucking, thrashing her legs out as he continued to drive his hips forward. Calling her name over and over again. Until he was tumbling with her, his body stiffening behind her as he ground out her name one last time.

Her chest heaved as she gasped for air, and she felt him chuckle behind her. "That was verra nice."

She couldn't help but laugh in agreement. "Aye. 'Twas indeed."

It seemed to take them longer to catch their breaths this time, but soon, her lids grew heavy and she slipped into a dreamless oblivion, Finlay's scent and arms enveloping her.

When she woke later, she was unsure of the time. Finlay slept soundly beside her. He was on his stomach, his arm draped around her waist. For a moment, she listened to his soft breathing and studied his handsome features in the waning light of the fire, burning them into her mind's memory. At some point during the night, he must have gotten up and added logs to the fire for it to still be going.

Careful not to wake him, she gingerly extracted herself from his arm and slipped from the bed. Quietly, she gathered her things and dressed as best she could without making a racket and waking Finlay. Pulling her cloak on, she tied it around the neck and grabbed her overnight bag.

Looking back at the bed, her heart threatened to shatter into a thousand pieces. She took a deep breath and grasped the doorknob, pausing for another look. Her emotions warred within her. She was leaving the only man she had ever loved. Aye, loved. She knew that now.

If she didn't walk out the door now, she never would. But it was hard mustering up the courage to walk away forever. She had finally found someone that made her happy, only to have him cruelly ripped away from her. Fate was a fickle thing.

Needing to make haste and worried that she was losing the courage to do what was right, she pushed open the door. The loud creak echoed through the room and she froze, daring a look at Finlay, but he still slept peacefully, undisturbed.

He was going to be so angry when he woke. Mayhap even hurt. But it was the right thing to do. He would eventually find someone to love. The thought made her insides scream, but she couldn't be selfish. She had to do what was right for Finlay.

Closing the door behind her, Willamina made her way down the hall and the two flights of stairs. A wall clock struck six times. She had slept in later than she wanted to. All due to how sated Finlay made her feel. And she would never forget the feeling of sleeping beside him, his strong arms wrapped around her body, his nose nuzzled into her neck.

She shook her head. These thoughts would serve her no purpose right now. The man that had checked them in the previous night entered from one of the back rooms at the sound of Willamina's descent.

"My lady, is something amiss?" he asked, concern creasing his forehead.

"Nay," she answered, shaking her head as she set down her bag. "Do ye have paper and quill, sir?"

"Of course, one moment."

Taking a seat in one of the stuffed chairs, she folded her hands in her lap, unable to stop herself from looking at the stairs. She half expected to see Finlay come running down them.

When the innkeeper returned with the items she'd asked for, she thanked him, and scribbled a quick note to Finlay. She couldn't just leave with no explanation to him. Guilt and shame flooded through her already. She didn't need to add more stress to the situation.

Folding the note in a neat square, she wrote Finlay on the front, then removed a ribbon from her hair and tied it around the paper.

She handed the note to the man and returned the ink and quill. "Can you ensure that Lord Primrose gets this note when he comes down later this morn?"

The innkeeper's eyes narrowed at her request, but he nodded and took the note from her hand, putting it into a nearby drawer.

"Thank ye." And with that, she walked out of the inn, each step taking her further and further from Finlay. From the life they could have had.

The life they should have had.

TEARS STREAKED WILLAMINA'S cheeks as she opened the door to Warton House. Harold greeted her in the entryway and took her bag.

"My lady, Sir Watson is in the study."

She pressed her lips together and nodded, not trusting herself to say anything. Her eyes darted down the hall that would lead her to Gerard's study. Afore, she had never been allowed in the room. It was his private sanctuary he would tell her.

With heavy feet, she moved down the hall, swiping at the tears. She paused outside the door and took a deep breath. She wanted answers. He didn't want her as a wife, she knew that. He didn't before, why would he now?

Then there was the matter of Lady Esmerelda. Something had been nipping at the edge of her mind about the woman. Had she and Gerard worked together to run her out of the city? To cause such a scandal that she would be shunned?

None of it made sense. There were much quicker ways to get rid of one's wife. It was rare, but there was divorce. He could have shunned her himself instead of planning this ruse.

She shook her head to clear it and straightened her shoulders and with one final deep breath, she pushed the door open.

Gerard's sneer let her know that he was fully expecting to see her. He didn't get up from his desk. He just sat there with that stupid look upon his face as he eyed her up and down.

"Wife," he greeted.

"Dinna call me that."

He had the nerve to look affronted as he grasped at his heart. "That hurts, Willamina. Truly."

"Ye ne'er called me that when we were married, dinna do so now."

"Ah," he stood and came around his desk, stopping in front of her and putting his hands on her upper arms. "See, lest ye forget. We are still married."

She shivered at his touch, disgust plain on her face as she shook his hands away.

"I am no' the woman I was when ye," she searched for the right words, "when whate'er 'tis ye did. I only want to know why. Why such a grand ruse? What did ye get out of it?"

"Ye're right. I ne'er called ye wife, because I ne'er wanted ye as my wife to begin with. Your parents had approached me with the proposition years before. If I had known ye would have grown to be such a bore, I would have rejected the offer straightaway."

His words were like a dagger to her heart, slicing away at the walls she had built around herself in the time he'd been gone. Each word a stab meant to inflict more pain.

"Ye could have divorced me."

He laughed. A deep bellow that echoed in the room. "And lose part of my estate? Absolutely no'." Shaking his head he walked to his desk, leaning on it and crossing his ankles. "Your parents and I had a deal."

Her eyes narrowed. "What do my parents have to do with this?"

"E'erything. They have e'erything to do with this. They helped hatch the plan." He laughed at the shock on her face.

"I dinna believe ye."

He shrugged. "It doesna matter if ye do or no'."

She shook her head, refusing to believe what he said. "Why would they do such a thing?"

"Coin. Your parents were always a greedy lot."

He wasn't wrong there. She and her parents were never close and more often than not they treated her like a bartering tool. She remembered the horror she felt when they told her she would be marrying Gerard. They gave her no choice and forced her into the union. No matter how many times she tried to tell her mother how miserable she was, the conversations went nowhere.

"They were supposed to hold my funds then revert them back to me. Their untimely deaths wrecked that plan. Literally," he chuckled, alluding to their carriage accident.

The man was vile.

"Who knew ye had a long-lost cousin. 'Twould have been so much easier without him and his interference."

"I will go to the courts."

He scoffed. "And say what?"

"I will tell them what ye've done."

"Dearest Willamina. Ye really are a naive twit. 'Tis no' criminal for me to have an accident in the water and wash up on a faraway shore. It took time for me to make my way home. Especially when I couldna recall my name."

"Ye lie."

"Ye have no proof to the contrary."

She couldn't believe what she was hearing. The past year and a half flooded her mind. Her year of mourning. Her parents' sympathy over the loss of her husband. Their deaths. The medium scandal that forced her to leave. Yet, through it all, she knew he was right. No one would believe her. Her mind wandered to Finlay. He should be awake by now. Her stomach churned at the pain and deceit he was more than likely feeling.

Strong, handsome Finlay. He stood up for her. Actually *loved* her.

And Gerard had ruined it all.

"Gerard?" A sleepy voice called from the hall.

"Come in, love." His eyes slammed into Willamina's when he called the woman 'love'. A cruel sneer ticked up the corners of his mouth.

The door opened and the woman that had ruined her life as she'd known it entered. Gone were the ridiculous clothes, and over the top head dress, and gaudy jewelry. There were no billowing robes flowing behind her.

The woman went over to Gerard and kissed him full on the lips, letting her hand flutter over his crotch. He pulled her close and sucked on her earlobe, never taking his eyes off Willamina.

"Willamina, I believe ye've already met Esme."

Willamina jutted her chin out, refusing to let Gerard see how upset she was. "Aye," she snapped back. "Though I believe she went by Esmerelda back then."

Esme, as she was now called, had the gall to laugh. Just threw her head back and laughed at the top of her lungs as she snaked her arms around Gerard's neck.

"I assume ye being a medium was all a ruse as well?"

The woman rolled her eyes. "That seance nonsense is such a scheme. Talking to the dead. I mean, really. 'Twas too easy to draw ye in."

Willamina backed toward the door, shaking her head. She was a fool. A stupid, stupid fool.

THE EARLY MORNING light streaming through the drapes and directly into Finlay's face woke him up from one of the best nights of sleep he had had for as long as he could remember.

Memories of the events of the previous night and early morning hours flooded his mind and his body roared to life. He smiled and stretched his arm to draw Willamina close, the need to bury himself deep strong, but his hand found naught but the mattress.

He sat up, looking at the empty bed.

"Mina," he called, gazing around the room. He didn't see her. She wasn't here. He shoved the covers off him and jumped out of bed, checking the floor to make sure she hadn't fallen or something. His breath caught in his throat when his eyes landed on his overnight bag. Only his bag was there. Hers was gone.

"Nay," he said aloud to the empty room as he grabbed his trousers and hurriedly pulled them on. His boots followed, and then his shirt. Where the hell had she gone?

He thought of what happened between them the night before. What they had shared. Had he scared her away? His mind searched for some kind of hint that her plan was to leave all along.

He found none.

Confused and devastated, he left the room, not caring that he certainly looked a mess. He convinced himself that mayhap she was breaking her fast early in the dining room. Though he knew it was a lie. She wouldn't take her bag to eat her eggs.

He practically ran down the stairs as worry edged into his brain. What if something horrible happened to her?

The innkeeper met him at the bottom of the stairs. "My lord. I have been asked to personally deliver this to ye."

Finlay snatched the note from his hand, immediately noticing the ribbon. It was Willamina's. She had worn it on the first day of their trip on the way to Inverness.

Untying the ribbon, he unfolded the paper and read the words that shattered his heart.

Dearest Finlay,

I must apologize for not saying goodbye. I knew if I did, I would never be able to leave. Thank ye for the memories of last night. Thank ye for showing me what it felt like to be loved. I will forever treasure them and ye in my heart and mind. Ye will soon forget about me and find yourself a proper wife, as ye should have done from the beginning. Now ye can do so. Our marriage is void, so 'tis like it never happened. I am sorry for any pain caused, but please know 'tis for the best.

Mina

The roar that burst through his chest had the innkeeper running back into the room. "My lord?"

"My wife. What time did she leave?"

"I-I," the man stuttered.

"What time?" he asked again, his voice deathly low.

"Just after six, my lord."

"By carriage?"

The man shook his head, shrugging his shoulders. "I dinna ken, my lord. I did no' watch her after she closed the door."

"Hold our room until I return. I dinna ken when that will be, but ye will be compensated well."

"Aye, my lord."

Finlay barely heard the innkeeper's answer as he was already out the door, looking down one side of the road and then the other side as if he would get a glimpse of her.

He cursed. He never slept in late. The one time he did was the time Willamina upped and left. She had two hours on him. She had to have gone to Warton House.

Why the hell would she want to go back there? Especially after what Gerard had done to her. But where else would she go?

He called for a carriage and waited for what seemed like hours for it to arrive, though it was only minutes. He rattled off the address to Warton House, telling the driver to make haste, and jumped into the carriage. The whole ride worry for Willamina consumed him. Along with why. Over and over again, his mind kept asking the same question.

It made no sense. She had never loved Gerard.

She never loved him either, he reminded himself. She'd never returned the sentiment when he confessed to her the previous night.

Nay, he refused to believe that she didn't have any feelings for him. She may not have voiced them, but they were there. In the way she looked at him. The way her eyes followed his movements. The lilt to her voice when she spoke to him. The passion in her kisses.

And last night. There was absolutely no way naught of that was real. It wasn't an act.

The carriage jostled along and he willed the horses to go faster.

He just had to get to her. To make her see that the past didn't matter. Gerard didn't matter. Whatever his reasoning was for what he did, it didn't matter. They could move forward and forget about Inverness. Go back to Edinburgh and build a life together.

He pushed his hands through his hair in frustration at how long the ride was taking. Anger and worry consumed him, warring within him. Anger at Gerard, the piece of shite, and worry that Willamina, in trying to fix things, was only going to make matters worse.

What if he got to Warton House and Willamina wasn't there? What then? And it hit him then. No matter how much time he and Willamina had spent together these last few weeks, there was much he didn't know about her. She was still a mystery.

One that he would gladly solve if she gave him the chance. His heart ached. Worse than that. It felt like it had been ripped from his chest.

The carriage jolted to a stop and he jerked forward. Seeing Warton House outside the window, he pushed the door open and jumped out of the carriage. Running to the door, he pounded his fist on the wood, not caring if he woke up the whole damn neighborhood.

CHAPTER TWENTY

A T THE SOUND of banging and then yelling, Willamina looked toward the study door.

Gerard swore and pushed Esme away from him most unceremoniously and left the room, Willamina close on his heels.

Harold was hurrying toward them, and behind him, eyes ablaze, Finlay was charging down the hall. "Mina!"

She couldn't help it. Forget the promises she'd made to herself that she would let him go. She ran to him, closing the distance until he wrapped his strong arms around her and she nuzzled into the warmth of his neck.

He hugged her like she was his world and she clung to him for dear life. Pulling his head away, he assessed her. "Are ye well?" He brushed her hair back from her face, his eyes crinkled with concern as he waited for her to answer.

She nodded. "I am fine."

"Isna that sweet? Get out of my house!" Gerard demanded, pointing down the hall.

Finlay extricated himself from Willamina's arms and held her at his side. "I dinna ken what ye've discussed this morn, but I need to speak to my wife."

"She isna your—"

"My wife," Finlay growled. "I will speak with her in private. I am no' leaving until I do."

Gerard seemed to get his wits about him and nodded stiffly. "Ye may have the library," he finally ceded, before turning on his heel and disappearing down the hall.

"What are ye doing here?" She asked, but he only shook his head as they made their way to the library.

Shutting the door behind them, Willamina didn't know what to say. Or where to look. The pain etched on Finlay's face was heartbreaking. And she got the sense that he was barely containing a simmering rage.

His eyes burned into hers. "Ye left."

Those two words hung in the air. Heavy and sad.

She pressed her lips together, and took a deep breath through her nose, before collapsing into a chair. "I had to."

"The hell ye did," he snapped.

"I left ye a letter," she whispered.

"Och, I got it. I didna understand it." He shook his head. "No' after last night. What we shared. Did it mean naught to ye?" His voice broke with the pain pulsing through him.

"It meant e'erything to me, Finlay. Ye made me feel things I had only dreamt about." She couldn't stop wringing her hands in her lap.

"Then why did ye run?"

The pain lancing his voice was hard to hear. She closed her eyes against it. "For ye. I ran for ye."

He laughed. A maniacal laugh sounding like naught she had ever heard from him before. "Nay," he said, shaking his head. "Ye didna leave for me. If 'twas for me, ye would have stayed."

"Finlay," she said softly, trying to figure out how to explain to him her actions. "Our marriage isna real. We said that from the beginning."

"Things changed between us. Ye canna deny it. I ken ye felt it, too."

Her heart was shattering because he was right. She had. But it didn't change the circumstances they now found themselves in.

"Ye are right. But e'erything has changed now. Our marriage on paper isna e'en real now. It canna be. But," she took a deep breath and continued. "We still accomplished what we planned.

Ye have your title. I hope ye are able to keep it. If no', ye are free to make another pact with another woman. 'Tis what ye wanted."

"Damn my title, Mina. 'Tis ye I want. Ye I long for. Ye that I dream about at night."

"But I am already married—"

"There is no' one court in all of Scotland that would consider ye still married to that bastard out there," he spat. "Ye had his death certificate, did ye no'?"

She nodded. "I did. I do. I," she pushed off the chair and began pacing the room, wringing her hands in front of her.

"That is all ye need to prove our marriage is true."

She shook her head in denial. "Why would ye want to continue? Ye have what ye want."

"Nay, nay I dinna. Without ye by my side, I dinna have what I want. Nor what I need. Mina," he approached her and grabbed her arms, forcing her to stop pacing and face him. Forcing her to look into his eyes. "I love ye."

She just kept shaking her head, as her heart shattered ever further. "I have naught to offer ye," she whispered.

"What are ye talking about?" His eyes searched hers and she just wanted to collapse into a heap on the floor and cry for her situation.

"I have no estate. No money. No land. I have naught. With Gerard alive, he regains the notes to e'erything."

He grasped her arms harder, shaking her as if trying to get her to wake up from whatever state she was in. "I dinna give a damn about any of those things. I only need ye. Naught else. Just ye."

She saw it then. Saw the love swirling in the depths of his ice-blue eyes. Felt it in the way he was holding her, and her breath left her in a rush.

"We can go home to Rosewood Manor. To Primrose Castle. They are yours as well as mine. We will speak with Bigsby. Have him draw up the paperwork ensuring that our marriage is legitimate. We dinna need Warton House. Let Gerard have it. Ye dinna need these bad memories. Let us create new ones. Happy ones. Together."

He crushed her in a hug so tight she could feel the beat of his heart through his jacket. His warmth enveloped her, and his arms felt like home. She clung to him like a life line. He was right. She didn't need Warton House. She didn't have anything when she'd married Gerard. And when she thought about it, she didn't want anything that would remind her of him. Of their horrible marriage.

She pulled away and met Finlay's eyes and she saw the worry in them. Guilt flooded her for hurting him so. She really thought she was doing what was best for him. But she saw it now. He was her future.

Lifting on her tiptoes, she wrapped her arms around his neck and pulled him down for a kiss. It was tender at first, before deepening. They let all of their emotions out in that lingering, soul-crushing kiss.

And then she let the words slip from her mouth. The words that she had been thinking, but trying to tamp down. But there was no denying them. Not any longer.

"I love ye, Finlay Primrose."

THE RIDE BACK to Edinburgh was done at their leisure, stopping for two nights on the way to not make the trip as stressful. It also gave Finlay time to show Willamina just how very much he loved her. Which he did, every chance he got.

Right now, they were back in the carriage, and only wicked thoughts were running through his mind. They'd just left the inn they spent their second night in and though they'd hardly slept, his body hungered for more.

Drawing the curtains to block out the outside world, he smiled at Willamina's look of surprise and waggled his eyebrows.

"'Twill be hours afore we arrive home," he said, his voice husky as he slid his hands up her legs, letting his fingertips flit over the soft skin of her thighs.

Her breath hitched as she watched him, her lip caught between her teeth, her eyes hooded and darkening with desire.

Sitting back on the opposite seat, he brought her with him and settled her onto his lap. "Kiss me, love."

A wicked glint lit her eyes and she licked her lips before capturing his mouth in a kiss, her tongue seeking entry into his and he obliged, their tongues twisting together in a wicked dance. His hands squeezed her buttocks through her gown and he ground his hips up, knowing she could feel the hard length of him at the apex of her thighs.

He fumbled for the buttons of his trousers, freeing himself, and then lifted her skirts, shifting their bodies so they aligned perfectly, and then sank himself into her sweet heaven.

She cried out, throwing her head back, her mouth open in ecstasy. He ran his tongue along the column of her neck as she lifted her hips up and down. Riding him, setting an excruciating pace that she knew drove him crazy.

Lips on his again, she ground her hips on him, taking him as far as she could, and he bucked. The little minx. She knew exactly what she was doing. He could tell from her smile that he felt against his mouth. Then she licked his ear, feathering kisses down his neck, and bit.

That was all it took to send him reeling, ready to tumble over the edge. He wanted her there with him.

He bucked his hips up, lifting his buttocks off the seat meeting her thrust for thrust and her whimpering cries let him know she was close. When she started tightening around his cock, he bent his head and sucked her turgid nipple into his mouth, nipping it and that was all she needed. She cried out his name as she stiffened on him and he pumped his hips, getting to where he needed.

Panting as he emptied himself into her. Their breaths ragged.

Chests heaving.

Her eyes fixed on his. "Do ye think the coachman heard us?" She asked finally, feigning innocence with a wicked gleam in her eye.

"Och, aye. I believe the wildlife did as well." He winked at her before lifting her off him and straightening her gown as best he could, then tucked himself away and fastened his trousers.

"I've ne'er passed the time in a carriage like that afore. Lord Primrose, ye are opening up a whole new world to me," she giggled, settling beside him after pushing the curtain open so they could once again see outside.

"Always glad to be of service, my lady."

"Now," she said, tapping her chin. "How do we spend the rest of the journey?"

The look on her face was pure lust. "Ye are a wicked one, love. Ne'er change."

"I willna."

"Promise?" He asked.

"With all my heart."

CHAPTER TWENTY-ONE

SEVERAL DAYS LATER, Finlay once again found himself sitting in the Rosebery solicitor's office, only this time, instead of Fingal in the other chair, it was Willamina. His twin had left shortly after they returned and hadn't been back since. No doubt deep in his cups in one of the whorehouses in town, Yvette a distant memory.

Willamina looked beautiful in her green gown with cap sleeves and a tartan sash. Her brown hair was swept up into a bun. Her cheeks were flushed, though that more than likely had to do with their little excursion on their way to the Bigsby's house.

They had been back in Edinburgh for a week. And most of that time had been spent in their bedchamber ignoring the rest of the world. How he wished they could spend the rest of their days there, focused on no one but themselves.

Even now, sitting here waiting to talk to Bigsby, the only thing on his mind was leaving here and losing himself in Willamina as soon as they got back home—if they lasted that long.

It was a week of them learning every inch of each other. Talking of their dreams. What they wanted their future to look like.

"My lord, lady. I apologize for the delay." Bigsby swept into the room, his brow damp with sweat that he wiped with his handkerchief. He looked like he'd been running. "I had an appointment on the other side of the city that went longer than expected."

He opened the large folder he'd carried in under his arm and spread the contents on the desk. He slipped on a pair of spectacles to study the pages laid out before him.

Finlay grasped Willamina's hand and squeezed. She looked nervous now that Bigsby had arrived.

"All is in order, I presume?" Finlay asked.

Nodding, the man didn't look up from his desk. "It appears to be." He held up a document and handed it to him. "Sir Watson has signed stating that he doesna contest your marriage and that since he was presumed deceased, Lady Primrose was within her rights to re-marry."

Willamina audibly let out a breath. They'd both been worried that the louse wouldn't keep his word. Of course, it helped that she sought no claim to any land or holdings belonging to Watson. He could go on his merry way. Mystery still surrounded why he had done what he'd done in the first place, but it mattered naught.

"That is great news. Is there anything further ye need from us?

"Just Lady Primrose's signature here," he pointed to the bottom of the document, "agreeing that the union is dissolved, and she will no' be seeking anything further from Sir Watson."

Willamina scoffed at the statement. "I will sign. I have no need for anything from my former husband."

Bigsby handed her an inked quill and she signed where instructed, and they were done.

He stood and shook hands with Bigsby. "Thank ye. I've seen ye more this past year than I have in the previous ten. I hope we can get back to that schedule," he chuckled as he held his hand out to help Willamina up.

"Aye, my lord. I must agree." He gathered up the documents and slid them back in the folder. "I bid a good day to ye both. Congratulations again on your marriage."

Outside, the air was cool and the wind grew strong, forewarning an incoming storm. Willamina clutched her cloak tighter around her neck as they waited for their carriage.

"I canna wait to get ye home," he nipped at her ear once they were inside the carriage, bumping along the road on the way back to Primrose Castle.

And he couldn't. He thought back to just a couple of months before. If he had denied Northington's party request, he would have never met Willamina. The thought of not having her in his life now was unfathomable.

She'd enriched his life in so many ways. And now he understood why Nicholas and Alexander were so besotted whenever they thought of their wives. He was the same way with Willamina. He couldn't imagine a day without her by his side.

Mayhap his father knew what he was doing when he added that clause to his will. It brought him to Willamina. What he thought was a curse that would lead him to misery turned out to be just the opposite.

"What are ye thinking about so seriously?" Willamina asked, concern furrowing her brows.

He smiled, kissing the top of her head. "I am thinking about how I am the luckiest man alive. And how I have my father to thank for that."

She placed a hand on his heart and patted, tilting her face up to meet his. "There really is no other like ye, Fin."

When he captured her mouth, he poured all of his emotions into that kiss. He wanted her to feel how much she meant to him.

And the way she melted against him let him know she did. He savored her lips and held her close, never wanting to let her go.

It was the best feeling in the world.

"I love ye, lass, more than ye can e'er ken."

She gave him a shy smile, her eyes filled with love, reflecting back the same feelings he had.

He could get lost in those eyes.

The carriage jolted to a stop and he grinned. "We're home."

This time, when they walked through the door, there were no more worries that something or someone could barge in and ruin their solace.

There was hope and happiness.

But most importantly, there was love.

He was the luckiest man in the world and he would spend the rest of his days ensuring Willamina knew that.

EPILOGUE

One Year Later

WILLAMINA COULDN'T CONTAIN her excitement. She, Gwen, and Clarissa were gathered in the salon at Rosewood Manor. They sat at a table that had been set in the center of the room, an oil lamp in the middle glowed low. Incense burned and their eyes were all focused on the woman sitting in front of them, shuffling the cards that would tell them their futures.

It wasn't a seance. As much as she enjoyed hosting them before the whole Gerard and Esmerelda fiasco, she didn't want to revisit them. The past was the past. She couldn't change it and there was no one that she wanted to contact.

But their future? Now that was wide open. The women were giddy as they eagerly awaited Fiona to flip the cards that would give them some insight into what they could look forward to.

Gwen was first and clapped her hands in delight as she learned that Nicholas would successfully create a hybrid orchid that would bring him much notoriety.

"He will love that," she said proudly. "He spends so much time in his greenhouse, mixing seeds, caring and cultivating them. Thank ye."

"Your grace," Fiona addressed Clarissa. "Your wool harvest this year will be one for the record books, setting ye and your family for years to come."

Tears welled in Clarissa's eyes. It was just last year when they almost lost their flock of sheep and to hear that the Campbell wool harvest would be more successful than projected was a welcome relief.

"Congratulations," Willamina said, squeezing Clarissa's hand. "Now, Lady Primrose."

Willamina straightened as Fiona studied the cards laid out before her on the table. The woman tilted her head to the left, then the right, still looking at the cards intently. "Ye have no wee bairns yet, nay?"

Willamina's shoulders sagged. It wasn't for lack of trying on her and Finlay's part. Heaven knows they had done more than their fair share, but to no avail so far. She shook her head. "Nay, no' yet."

Fiona smiled. "'Tis the correct answer—no' yet. Ye shall soon, dinna fash."

Her hopes soared at the thought. Could Fiona be right? She desperately wanted to believe so.

Later that night, after everyone said their goodbyes and left, and Finlay and Willamina settled into bed, he pulled her into his strong arms, wrapping her in his warmth. Fiona's words kept playing over and over in her head.

"What has ye mind so preoccupied, love?" He kissed her forehead and waited for her answer.

She wasn't sure if she should tell him. She worried that he was upset that she hadn't conceived yet. A year was a long time to not be with a bairn.

"Our future family," she confessed.

His eyebrows shot up. "Do ye have news?"

She shook her head. "Nay, no' yet."

"Well, then," he said, covering her body with his. "I think we should rectify that." In an instant, he disappeared under the covers, working her body into a heated frenzy and just as she was about to explode, he kissed his way up her body. Nipped her neck and sank himself deep with a groan. "Heaven. Ye feel like heaven," he said, pumping his hips.

She wrapped her legs around his back, pulling on his buttocks, urging him deeper. He obliged. Rocking back and forth, working her nerves into a frenzy and when he knew she was close, slipping his hand between them and circling the little bundle of nerves through her nestle of curls.

And she was done. Exploding out a release that had her screaming his name as stars shone behind her eyes and her breaths came in short gasps.

He was right there with her, pumping faster and faster, until he slammed into her a final time, swelling even more within her as he emptied his seed into her, stiff as he ground out her name, and she felt it.

Something different.

She just knew it. Her courses wouldn't come.

They'd just created a life.

And she couldn't wait to meet the wee one as she pictured a boy with the same handsome looks as his father. Or a daughter with those same ice-blue eyes and her hair color.

It didn't matter which. Just knowing that it had finally happened was all she needed.

"I love ye," she whispered.

"No' as much as I love ye," he countered, gathering her in his arms.

And in his arms is where she slept, with a smile on her lips, as she dreamt of their future family.

About the Author

Award-winning author Brenna Ash is addicted to coffee, chocolate, and all things Scotland and BTS. She's a firm believer that one can never have too much purple or glitter. She loves rom-coms and always cries at the HEAs.

When she's not busy writing about sexy, Scottish Highlanders, Medieval Pirates, Regency Rogues, or co-hosting the true crime podcast, Crime Feast, she spends her time reading with her favorite music playing in the background, binge-watching Outlander and Bridgerton, park-hopping with her besties, spoiling her cat, Lilly, or watching BTS content online. Brenna lives with her husband on the Space Coast in sunny Florida.

Website – www.brennaash.com
Amazon – amazon.com/stores/author/B01H46ZA02
Facebook – facebook.com/BrennaAshAuthor
Instagram – instagram.com/brennaashauthor
BookBub – bookbub.com/profile/brenna-ash

www.ingramcontent.com/pod-product-compliance
Lightning Source LLC
Chambersburg PA
CBHW060450310726

48977CB00001B/384

* 9 7 8 1 9 6 5 5 3 9 1 2 5 *